IT HAPPENED ON A TRAIN

BRIXTON BROTHERS

IT HAPPENED ON A TRAIN

BY
Mac Barnett

ILLUSTRATIONS BY
Adam Rex

SIMON & SCHUSTER BOOKS FOR YOUNG READERS
New York • London • Toronto • Sydney • New Delhi

SIMON & SCHUSTER BOOKS FOR YOUNG READERS
An imprint of Simon & Schuster Children's Publishing Division
1230 Avenue of the Americas, New York, New York 10020
This book is a work of fiction. Any references to historical events, real people, or real locales are used fictitiously. Other names, characters, places, and incidents are products of the author's imagination, and any resemblance to actual events or locales or persons, living or dead, is entirely coincidental.
Text copyright © 2011 by Mac Barnett
Illustrations copyright © 2011 by Adam Rex
All rights reserved, including the right of reproduction in whole or in part in any form.
SIMON & SCHUSTER BOOKS FOR YOUNG READERS is a trademark of Simon & Schuster, Inc.
For information about special discounts for bulk purchases, please contact Simon & Schuster Special Sales at 1-866-506-1949 or business@simonandschuster.com.
The Simon & Schuster Speakers Bureau can bring authors to your live event. For more information or to book an event, contact the Simon & Schuster Speakers Bureau at 1-866-248-3049 or visit our website at www.simonspeakers.com.
Also available in a Simon & Schuster Books for Young Readers hardcover edition
Book design by Lizzy Bromley
The text for this book is set in Souvenir.
The illustrations for this book were rendered digitally with a Wacom tablet and Photoshop CS3.
Manufactured in the United States of America
0813 OFF
First Simon & Schuster Books for Young Readers paperback edition September 2012
4 6 8 10 9 7 5 3
The Library of Congress has cataloged the hardcover edition as follows:
Library of Congress Cataloging-in-Publication Data
Barnett, Mac.
It happened on a train / Mac Barnett ; illustrations by Adam Rex. — 1st ed.
p. cm. — (Brixton Brothers)
Summary: Seventh-grader Steve Brixton finds himself pulled back into sleuthing when, during a train trip down the California coast, he uncovers a mystery involving a fleet of priceless automobiles, an assassin, and a private rail car.
ISBN 978-1-4169-7819-0 (hardcover)
[1. Railroad trains—Fiction. 2. Robbers and outlaws—Fiction. 3. California—Fiction. 4. Mystery and detective stories. 5. Humorous stories.] I. Rex, Adam, ill. II. Title.
PZ7.B26615It 2011
[Fic]—dc22
2011009114
ISBN 978-1-4169-7820-6 (pbk)
ISBN 978-1-4424-2313-8 (eBook)

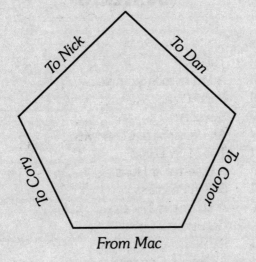

To Nick

To Dan

To Cory

To Conor

From Mac

CONTENTS

Contents

Contents

IT HAPPENED ON A TRAIN

CHAPTER I

THE END

IT WAS WEDNESDAY EVENING, a.k.a. trash night. Steve Brixton, seventh grader, formerly of the Brixton Brothers Detective Agency, plodded along his driveway, dragging a maroon bin behind him. The bin's wheels rumbled and popped as they rolled over pebbles on the blacktop. This week the Brixton family's bin was very full. The lid would not close tightly; it bounced up and down, making an irregular, slow clapping sound. And the trash was heavy—Steve could feel the can's weight in his elbow, and he kept switching the arm he used to drag it: right, then left, and back again. He sighed. Tonight was a particularly difficult trash night, and that's because the garbage bin contained fifty-nine shiny, red-backed books: a complete set of the Bailey Brothers Mysteries, a series of detective novels that until a week and a half ago had been Steve's favorite books of all time.

Steve pulled the bin down off the curb. It hit the street hard, and its lid bounced open like a clam's shell, revealing the can's contents. Steve stood underneath a streetlamp. Its orange bulb flickered and hummed, even though the sun was just now setting and there was still plenty of light in the sky.

There they were, neatly stacked in a cardboard box atop a week's worth of kitchen scraps and dental floss: Bailey Brothers #1 to #58, and of course *The Bailey Brothers' Detective Handbook*, which was jam-packed with Shawn and Kevin Bailey's Real Crime-Solving Tips and Tricks. (Shawn and Kevin Bailey, as pretty much everybody knows, were the sons of world-famous detective Harris Bailey and the heroes of the Bailey Brothers books—they had their own crime lab and fixed their own cars and were basically the acest sleuths around.) The handbook had chapters full of things every serious gumshoe would need to know: stuff like "Tailing Baddies," "Making Your Own Blowgun," and "*Modus Operandi, Portrait Parlé*, and Other Funny Foreign Phrases for the American Sleuth."

Steve stood and stared at his books. He looked around. Identical maroon bins stood like sentries outside every home on the street. The neighborhood was quiet. Assured that he was alone, Steve reached out and picked up a book: Bailey Brothers #15: *The Phantom of Liar's Bluff*, which started like this:

CHAPTER II

A MYSTERIOUS SIGHTING

"Dad sure is busy with his new case," mused fair-haired Kevin Bailey as he piloted their sedan along the twists and turns of Bayside Road.

"I wonder if he'll let us help out with the sleuthing when he gets back from the Yukon," wondered his younger brother, Shawn, who had dark hair and was a better football player but slightly less handsome.

"Say, fellows, all this talk of work is making me hungry!" whined the

Baileys' stout chum Ernest Plumly, as he nibbled on a hoagie in the backseat.

"I would change the subject," needled Kevin, "but I'm having trouble thinking of a subject that *doesn't* make you hungry."

Shawn and Kevin broke into hearty, good-natured laughter. Ernest, who was almost as well known for his voracious appetite as he was for his loyalty to the Baileys, grinned ruefully. "You fellows can kid me all you want. It's all right. I've got this sandwich to keep me company. I call it the Ernest: shredded lettuce, chopped pickles, smoked ham, roast beef, tomatoes, horseradish, and the secret ingredient: five kinds of mustard."

"Just try not to get any crumbs on the upholstery," joked Kevin. He floored the accelerator, and the sedan tore around a blind curve. The boys spent much of their spare time souping up their Tucker Torpedo, and it was the finest car in Benson Bay. The roar of its engine belied the boys' affectionate nickname for the car: the Jalopy.

The car rounded another curve, and

the Baileys' boathouse appeared.

"There are the girls!" shouted Kevin. "Lay on the horn, why don't you!"

Cissie Merritt and Hannah Fenway waved excitedly when they heard the Jalopy's horn. Kevin often dated pretty, vivacious Cissie. Hannah, Cissie's quiet and doe-eyed best friend, was Shawn's favorite girl in Benson Bay (and the neighboring towns of Kelly Bay and Bayshore, too). The girls were both dressed in bathing suits and carried picnic baskets under their arms, ready for a day aboard the Baileys' speedboat, *The Deducer IV*. The first three *Deducer*s had all been spectacularly wrecked in the Baileys' previous crime-solving exploits.

"I'm so glad we're finally getting to

have this picnic," sang Cissie. "Our last day out was interrupted by that case you two cracked." She was referring to the time Shawn and Kevin busted a gang of carnies and criminal clowns and learned *The Secret Behind the Fun House Mirror.*

"Thanks for not being sore at having to reschedule," offered Shawn, unpacking the trunk. "We'll make it up to you gals on the water. Kevin may be a leadfoot behind the Jalopy, but wait till you see the tricks I can get up to in *The Deducer.*"

The youths laughed together.

"I'm just excited to try out my new present from my dad," beamed Ernest. Mr. Plumly was a prominent lawyer in Benson Bay.

"What did he give you?" asked Shawn.

"I'll give you two sleuths a hint. They're perfect for bird watching."

Ernest pulled a pair of high-powered binoculars out of his satchel.

Shawn and Kevin whistled appreciatively. "That sure is a swell pair of glasses," Kevin commented.

Ernest held the binoculars up to his eyes and peered at the cliffs in the distance. "I can see all the way across to Liar's Bluff from here."

"Say, when do we get a turn, Mr. Audubon?" Hannah smiled.

Ernest didn't say anything. He slowly lowered the binoculars, and his friends noticed that his usually ruddy face had gone pale.

"What's the matter, chum?" Kevin queried. "You look like you've seen a ghost."

"I think I just did!"

Steve's reading was interrupted by squealing brakes. A dented silver station wagon had stopped a few feet from his trash bin. A voice Steve had never heard before shouted, "There you are! I've been looking for you."

CHAPTER III

POINT PANIC

THE DRIVER'S FACE was gradually revealed as the wagon's grimy passenger-side window descended. Steve guessed he was in his late twenties. He had straight black hair and bright red sunglasses, even though it was dusk. A surfboard was tied to the roof of his car.

Steve's old instincts awoke somewhere near his belly.

Who wore sunglasses at this hour? Criminals, that's who. Also guys who tried too hard to look cool.

Steve looked back toward his house. If this guy tried anything funny, Steve could sprint to his front door in eight seconds. The man was probably harmless, but even a retired sleuth needed to be cautious. He took a closer look at the man's face, just in case he needed to give a description to the cops later. There was a streak of gray, weird for a guy that young, running back from his forehead. A sunburn was peeling near his temples, revealing bright pink skin underneath. And on his left cheek, just below the sunglasses, was a small birthmark in the shape of a pentagon.

The Bailey Brothers' Detective Handbook, which was now somewhere in Steve's trash, has some interesting things to say about birthmarks.

Sometimes successful sleuthing requires some amateur dermatology! The Baileys always pay attention to birthmarks. Red, black, or blue, birthmarks are often the key to cracking a case! Remember Bailey Brothers #26: *The Clue of the Rune in the Ruins*, when Shawn and Kevin unmasked a grave robber posing as the archaeologist Dr. David Franks after noticing the impostor lacked Franks's strawberry-shaped birthmark? It was ace! Of course, birthmarks are also a handy way to identify villainous Masters of Disguise, who often forget to conceal them. In fact many famous criminals have had interesting birthmarks! Here are just a few of the Baileys' favorite examples:

AL CAPONE
Right Thigh
Big Island of Hawaii

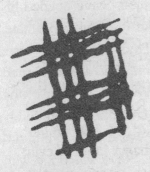

BILLY THE KID
Left Sole
Tartan of the MacDonald
Clan of Lochmaddy

BONNIE PARKER
Right Shoulder
Butterfly, or a Child Crying
Because His Dad
Forgot His Birthday

"Hey," said the man with the pentagonal birth-mark. "Aren't you Steve Brixton?"

"Yeah," said Steve.

The man looked pleased. "Nice! I was coming to see you! You're the famous detective, right?"

Steve shook his head. "I was. Now I'm retired. I just take out the trash for money."

The guy's jaw was slack. His hair hung lankly. "Oh."

After Steve Brixton's first case, *The Case of the Case of Mistaken Identity*, Steve's picture had been in several newspapers. Soon after, Steve opened his own detective agency, just like the Bailey Brothers, and things went terrifically. Until his second case. Steve uncovered *The Ghostwriter Secret* and learned that MacArthur Bart, his hero and the author of the Bailey Brothers books, was a criminal mastermind—who even tried to kill Steve. It was a thrilling but ulti-mately disorienting adventure. Steve was done with private detection. He'd shuttered his agency and started doing chores for ten dollars a week. It wasn't glamorous work, and it paid terribly.

"Why'd you retire?" the man in the car asked.

"It's a long story, but the short version is that nobody likes being lied to."

The man looked confused, probably because there

was no way he could know what Steve was talking about. Still, Steve had liked the way the sentence sounded.

The man brushed his hair out of his eyes, and it fell right back down. "I'm thinking maybe I could convince you to come back and solve one last case?"

"Sorry," said Steve. "I'm out for good."

"I think it's an interesting one."

"Nope."

The man looked at a scrap of paper in his hand. "You worked for the Brixton Brothers Detective Agency, right?"

"Yep."

"So what about your brother? Is he still a detective?"

"I'm an only child."

"Then why is it called—"

"It just sounds cooler, okay?"

"Chill, chill, little man. Look, how much did you charge, you know, back when you were a detective?"

"Two hundred dollars a day, plus expenses."

"I'll double it."

"Nope."

The man in the car seemed disappointed. This was obviously not how he had expected things to go. "Well you can still listen to me, right? I mean, I could tell you about what's going on?"

Steve shrugged. "It's a free country."

The man was encouraged. "Awesome. Okay, Steve—"

"Wait—what's your name?"

"Oh, sorry. I'm Danimal."

"Danimal?"

"Yeah, you know, short for Dan."

"You mean long for Dan."

"What?"

"Never mind."

Danimal was unfazed. "Okay, listen to this. So you know how Mímulo has been closed lately?"

"Yeah," Steve said. "The sharks, right?"

Mímulo Point was a popular surf break about fifteen minutes south of Ocean Park. A few weeks ago a longboarder had spotted a great white shark. More fins had been spotted since, and the area was closed to surfing and swimming. The local news shows had started calling Mímulo "Point Panic."

"Yeah. Sharks. It's brutal, 'cause Mímulo's my favorite spot."

Steve nodded. "Okay."

"But here's the thing—the thing is, I'm not actually scared of sharks. I mean, I wasn't. Because they don't really attack humans, right? I mean, I've got a buddy, a really smart guy, and he's always saying, 'Sharks

don't attack humans unless they think they're seals,'
right?"

"Sure," said Steve. Steve hated fish. And sharks
were the worst fish. Fish eyes never changed, and
looking at a fish—whether that fish was swimming in
the Ocean Park Aquarium or lying on a bed of ice
at some fancy buffet table—made you feel like you
didn't exist. But a shark—especially a great white—
would eat you, even while it refused to acknowledge
your existence, gazewise.

"So what I did was, I customized my wet suit with
like these green and orange patches on it. Right? So
now I don't look like a seal out there, when I'm sitting
in the lineup."

"Yep."

"Okay, so last night was a full moon, and I figured
nobody'd be watching the beach at night, and plus
the swell was super nice, and I wasn't afraid of sharks,
and so, well, I paddled out at Mímulo."

"What?"

Danimal was looking at Steve but not really seeing
him. His voice softened. "And I was attacked, man.
By a great white."

CHAPTER IV

SHARK ATTACK

"No!"

"Yeah."

"Wow."

"I know. I'd had a couple really good rides, and I was just sitting out there, right? It's peaceful, glassy; it's perfect. And the moon was right overhead. Just perfect. So quiet. And then suddenly—*wham!*—my board gets ripped out from under me. It was insane. Before I know it, I'm underwater and something's tugging—like, yanking—at my leash. And I'm getting dragged down hard, right? So this whole time I'm trying to get to my ankle strap, so I can release the board, but I'm freaking out, and the shark is just dragging that board down like a tombstone, and I'm just taking in mouthfuls of water, and—"

Steve clenched his jaw. He imagined himself in that water, pulled toward the sea floor, looking at that great white with its black and lolling eye.

"So finally I get to the ankle strap, and I rip it off. And my lungs are burning, and I have to swim up for air, but I don't even know which way is up. So I stay still, and I start to float up a little, and so then I start swimming up in that direction, and I finally break through the surface, and I'm just gasping for air."

"Yeah," said Steve.

"Okay, so I start swimming back to the beach, and all of a sudden there's this big whoosh and like a slap, and I look, and my board's come up. And I sort of pause, because I don't know whether to get it, because this shark must think it's a seal, right? But this is my favorite board—such a good board, and I really want to get it back, and I know this is dumb, but I swim over and get it, and I paddle like crazy back to the shore. And when I get to the beach, I see, well, check this out—"

Danimal hopped out of his car, loosened the ties on his roof rack, and pulled down a bright red long-board. Hopping around in his wet suit in the evening light, Danimal resembled nothing more than a harbor seal with green and orange patches. He brought his board in front of the car. Steve saw two jagged bites, one in the board's middle and the other down by the fins. Steve felt nauseated by the sight, but for some reason he couldn't stop looking.

"Did you report this?" Steve asked.

"No way. I wasn't supposed to be out there. I'm not getting in trouble."

"So what did you come here for?" Steve asked. "Was I supposed to track down the shark and teach him a lesson? I don't do hired muscle jobs, especially with great whites."

Danimal shook his head and laid the board down on the ground. "Nah. I want you to help me find a new place to surf."

"Why hire a private detective? Buy a map."

"No, no. I'm looking for a specific spot. A secret spot. In Baja. My grandfather used to surf it in the six-ties, and when I was a kid he used to tell me about a break only he knew about. Supposed to be the most consistent wave around—like a machine or some-thing, just pushing out perfect, peeling lefts for as long as you can see."

"I still don't see why you were looking for me," Steve said.

Danimal ducked into his car and pulled out a piece of paper. "Here's why: I was reading one of my grandpa's old books when I found this." He passed the scrap to Steve.

The paper was old and yellowed, and it felt brittle in Steve's hands. In the kind of handwriting nobody used anymore was written:

> Turn west at the south pole,
> go down, then climb over the
> old man who sleeps on the beach.
> Turn right and then walk
> to the place where the
> sea sings its own name.

Steve looked up. "So?"

"It's a riddle, man! A mystery. I want you to help me decipher this message and help me find the perfect wave."

Steve murmured. He took a walk around the surfboard to get his brain moving.

"So what do you say, Steve? Will you take the case?"

Steve stopped. "No."

Danimal was crestfallen.

"But I'll tell you this," Steve said, looking Danimal right in the eye. "Your story doesn't make any sense. You weren't attacked by a great white shark."

CHAPTER V

AN UNDERWATER CONSPIRACY

"ARE YOU CALLING ME A LIAR?" Steve couldn't make out
Danimal's face—the man was silhouetted in the car's
headlights—but he could tell Danimal was angry. "Did
you even look at my board? The evidence is right in
front of you."

"Exactly."

"Huh?"

"The evidence."

"Right."

"It's right in front of me."

"Yes."

"Yes."

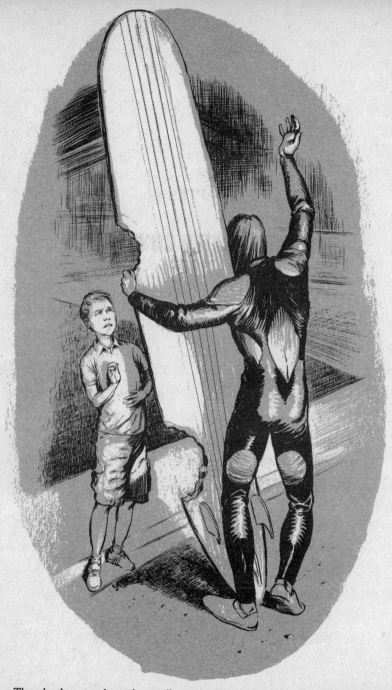

The shark-eaten board was illuminated by the wagon's headlights.

"What?"

Steve squinted in the glare (he wished he had a pair of sunglasses) and tried to smile. "Look, Danimal, I'm not saying you're lying. I believe you believe you were attacked by a shark, but I don't believe a shark attacked you."

"Dude. What are you talking about?"

"There are two big bites out of this board, right?"

"Yeah . . ."

"Well, that doesn't make any sense. Even if the shark thought your board was a seal, he'd know it wasn't after the first bite. So why would he take another mouthful of foam and fiberglass?"

Danimal stared.

"He wouldn't," Steve said. "Sharks don't do that."

"How do you know?"

Steve knew from watching a lot of TV shows about sharks. (It was important to understand the things you hated most.) He shrugged nonchalantly. "I used to be a detective. It was my job to know things."

Danimal was slowly nodding. "Okay . . . so then what bit my board?"

"Nothing. If I had to guess, I'd say you were attacked by a person. Someone wanted this to look like a shark attack to scare you off. And whoever it was overdid it." Steve was walking again, talking fast.

"I mean, it wouldn't be hard to rig up some sort of device that would make bite marks like a shark. Like one of those old bear traps, you know?" Steve felt a familiar glowing certainty right in his gut. "You know, I've got a hunch that all these great white sightings are fake. There are no sharks off Mímulo Point."

Danimal took a few seconds to respond, and when he did, his words came slowly. "Why would anyone fake a shark attack?"

Steve paced. Why? To get people out of the water. To cover up a crime. Smuggling. Trafficking. A secret search for underwater gold. Saboteurs targeting a nearby harbor. The clandestine construction of a submarine crime base. *Why wouldn't someone fake a shark attack?*

Steve made himself stand still. "None of my business," he said.

Danimal was excited. "What? Come on! There's a mystery here. Two mysteries. I'll pay you to figure this out *and* find my grandfather's secret surf spot. You can't pull out now, man. You've already broken the case wide open."

"I haven't done anything."

"Oh, now don't give me—"

"Look, Danimal. Take your story to the police. Ask for Chief Clumber. Maybe he can help you."

"The cops? You're seriously just going to give up? What about my grandpa's secret spot?"

"Your grandpa's note doesn't make any sense. There is no west at the south pole. At the south pole, every direction is north."

Danimal looked confused.

"Anyway," said Steve, "the south pole's not in Baja. It's in Antarctica. And I'm not going anywhere: My mom would kill me if I left Ocean Park again. I told you, Danimal. I retired. I'm just an ordinary kid now."

And with that, Steve turned around and walked back into his house.

CHAPTER VI

TOO MANY DANAS

"HEY, CH—" STEVE CAUGHT HIMSELF before he called his chum Dana a chum. "Chum" was a Bailey Brothers word, and he wasn't using it anymore. "Hey, buddy."

"Hey, Steve," said Dana.

On Thursday after school, Steve and his best friend, Dana, walked hands-in-pockets down the road that ran along the ocean, just like they always did.

And like she had for the past week, Dana's new girlfriend walked home with them.

Dana's new girlfriend was also named Dana, only her last name was Powers. Steve had always thought she was all right, until she and Dana started going out. Now it seemed like she was always around, and Steve found the combination of Dana and Dana vaguely but constantly irritating.

"Hey, Dana—," Steve said.

"What?" both Danas said at once, and then broke into near-identical laughter.

This had been going on a lot lately.

Steve turned to Dana Powers. "I didn't mean you. I meant Dana."

Dana sighed.

"I call you Other Dana, remember?" Steve said.

"Well *you're* the only one who calls me that, Steve," said Other Dana. "People have just been calling me Dana for twelve years, and you have been calling me Other Dana for like three days, so it's not like I have just reprogrammed my brain to not respond when I hear you say my name."

She had a good point. But Steve wasn't going to say so.

"Plus the whole Other Dana thing is so stupid," said Other Dana.

That was not a good point.

"Anyways—," said Other Dana.

That was another thing about Other Dana. She always said "anyways."

"—I don't see what the big deal is. We both have the same name. I think it's cute."

Steve scoffed. "Do you think it's cute, Dana?"

Dana shrugged glumly.

This whole situation was Steve's fault, really. Last Monday Dana had asked Steve to ask Other Dana to be his (Dana's) girlfriend. Steve said sure, no questions asked. Although there were a few questions he'd like to have asked, questions like, *Why do I have to do the asking again? And why do you want to be Dana Powers's boyfriend if you've never really talked to her for more than five minutes? And what exactly is entailed in being Dana Powers's boyfriend, anyway?*

That day, Dana Powers was standing at the top of a flight of stairs that led to the school's front entrance. She was surrounded by a group of five girls, and they were all laughing loudly. Dana Powers was laughing the loudest. Steve smoothed his hair and tried to control his breath as he started up the steps. On the fifth stair he caught Dana Powers's eye, but she turned right back to her friends. Steve rehearsed a script in his head—he imagined Dana P.'s surprise when she heard what Steve had to say. But his stomach was cold. Steve had felt this way before sometimes, when he was working on a case: Usually it meant he was walking into a trap.

He reached the group of girls. They'd gone quiet, but nobody was looking at Steve.

"Hey, Dana," he said, then lost his momentum.

Dana smiled encouragingly. She had a nice smile. "Yeah?"

"Can I talk to you for a second?" Steve swallowed. "Um, in private?"

Dana Powers smiled at her friends before she looked back at Steve. She sure was smiling a lot. "Yeah."

They shuffled a few feet over, Dana still on the top stair and Steve one below, until they reached the banister. She was wearing a sticker of a heart on her cheek, right below her left eye. Now her face was serious, and she looked at Steve closely, like she was recording the whole scene in her head to review again and again later.

"Um, you know my friend Dana?" Steve said. "Not you. I mean not that you're not my friend, but the guy who is like my best friend? Dana Villalon?"

"Uh-huh," she said without nodding. The heart was pink with a thin blue border.

"Do you want to be his girlfriend?" The words tumbled from Steve's mouth.

"Yeah," she said. Dana Powers was all smiles again as she skipped back over to her friends.

When Steve met Dana that day at the usual spot,

Dana was facing the ocean, but he couldn't have been watching the waves, because he had his palms pressed against his eyes. "Hey, chum," Steve said, and Dana didn't even correct him. He just looked at Steve, and Steve saw that his friend was scared. But when Steve delivered his report, Dana jumped high in the air, then lay down in the sandy dirt by the side of the road. Steve sat next to him for a while before they started back. That was the last time they walked home just the two of them.

Now everything was different. Other Dana was around all the time. And Other Dana was nothing like Cissie Merritt and Hannah Fenway, the Bailey Brothers' girlfriends. They only hung out with Shawn and Kevin when it was convenient for the brothers. And even then the girls spent most of their time sunbathing so Shawn and Kevin could go fly-fishing or explore suspicious rock formations.

"Have you started book four yet?" Other Dana asked.

"What?" Steve said.

"I wasn't talking—"

"Look at that," Dana said, pointing toward the beach. A flock of seagulls was dive-bombing an abandoned bag of french fries. The air was thick with birds, squawking and squabbling. One of the gulls managed to pick up the greasy bag and fly a few feet before another bird swooped down and knocked the prize from its beak. Fries fell and scattered on the sand, and the birds' shrieks grew loud and frantic. Steve and Dana laughed.

"*Anyways . . . ,*" said Other Dana, and then didn't say anything else.

"Anyway," said Steve.

"What?" said Other Dana, wheeling around on Steve so fast that he took an involuntary step back.

"It's anyway. Not anyways."

"What's your problem, Steve?" Other Dana said.

Steve wanted to say something, but he didn't have anything to say.

"Yeah. That's what I thought." Other Dana gave her head a disgusted shake. Then she turned around and walked away from the ocean, toward downtown Ocean Park.

The gulls kept squawking.

Dana watched her till she disappeared around a corner.

The boys kept walking.

"What's my problem?" Steve asked, forcing a laugh. "What's her problem, right?"

Dana was silent, then said quietly, "You could be nicer to her."

Unbelievable.

They walked without talking.

"You've been acting weird for a while," Dana said after a few minutes. "What's wrong? Still MacArthur Bart stuff?"

There was a lot wrong, but MacArthur Bart was probably the easiest to talk about.

"Yeah," Steve said. "Last night I put all my Bailey Brothers books in the trash—"

"Seriously?"

"I feel weird about them now. The guy who taught me everything I know about being a detective turned out to be a criminal mastermind—"

"Yeah, but that doesn't mean there's anything wrong with his books."

"I know, but—"

"I mean, he wrote all the Bailey Brothers books before he went bad, right?"

"Yeah."

"So look at it this way. Say MacArthur Bart was a wizard. And when he was young and innocent and good he wrote a famous book of spells. Then, when he got older, he was seduced by the dark arts and became an evil wizard. Just because he ended up becoming a dark mage doesn't mean that the grimoire that he wrote in his youth is evil too."

Steve was quiet for a few seconds. "When did you get so into wizards?"

"What?"

"Are you reading wizard books?"

"What? What are you talking about? I'm not so into wizards."

"Grimoire?"

"That's a wizard's spell book. Everybody knows that."

Steve stared at Dana. "Everybody does not know that."

"Whatever. I'm trying to help you. I don't know why you're making such a big deal about wizards."

"Um, I think you're the one making a big deal about wizards. Is this what Other Dana was talking about? Book four? Is she making you read wizard books?"

"She's not making me read them."

"So you are reading wizard books!"

"So what?"

"So you're changing is what. Come on, Dana. You're supposed to be the cool one."

Dana stopped walking. "What?"

Steve's face flushed, and he talked fast. "You're the cool one, Dana. You run faster, you go on nice trips with your parents, you read books about ships—"

"Oh, there aren't really any ships in these books. Wizards' magic doesn't work on water."

Steve slapped his forehead with two hands.

"What?" said Dana. "Look, they're not 'wizard books.' The third one doesn't even have wizards in it. It just has liches."

"What's a lich?"

"An undead wizard."

Steve groaned.

"What?" Dana asked.

"What's this series even called?"

Dana paused, then said quietly, "Wizards' Worlds."

"Wizards' Worlds."

"I'm serious. They're actually really good."

"Why didn't you tell me about this?"

"Are you joking? Do I have to tell you everything I'm reading? Do you want me to turn in a reading log every week?"

"No, but you were deliberately keeping these books a secret."

"Because I knew you'd react like this."

"Like what? I'm only upset because you were hiding stuff from me!"

"No. Not upset. I knew you'd make fun of me." Dana shook his head. "And I never made fun of your detective books."

Steve felt like he'd been punched in the solar plexus. "Why would you? There's nothing wrong with the Bailey Brothers books."

"Fine! That's what I was saying before you blew up about wizards."

Steve and Dana walked the rest of the way in silence.

When they got to Steve's street, they stopped.

"See you tomorrow," Steve said.

"Bye," said Dana.

Steve walked down Driftwood Avenue. What was Dana even talking about? How could he compare detective books and wizard books? That was dumb. And anyway, Steve hadn't really been making fun of Dana. Had he?

Steve opened the front door.

There was a man with a gun in his living room.

CHAPTER VII

A DISASTER AT HOME

THAT MAN WAS RICK ELLIOT, Steve's mom's boyfriend and Steve's number one enemy, especially now that Steve had stopped fighting crime. Rick was a cop, so the gun wasn't weird. Or illegal. Which was too bad. Steve would have loved it if Rick had committed a crime. Then he'd be in jail instead of Steve's living room.

"Stevie!" Rick said as Steve shut the front door. Lately Steve's mom, Carol, had been encouraging Rick and Steve to "become better friends." Since they weren't friends in the first place, it would be hard to become "better." Anyway, Stevie was Rick's new nickname for Steve, and Steve hated it.

Rick wore his boots, and his feet were on the couch while he watched a baseball game. Carol Brixton was always telling Steve to take off his shoes if he was going to lie on the couch. Did his mom not know about what was going on in here, or did Rick have some sort of exemption?

"Get your feet off the couch," Carol Brixton said, coming in from the kitchen. It took one look for Steve to realize that his mom was tired, and when she was tired, she went looking for arguments.

Rick gave Steve a conspiratorial glance, which was unreciprocated, and swung his legs over the couch's edge. When Rick turned back to the game, it looked like he was riding the sofa sidesaddle.

"Mute that," Carol said without looking at the TV. Rick did. "So," Carol said. "I called Mr. Meyer today to make sure your field trip was real. You know, it would be nice not to have to call your son's teacher all the time to make sure he wasn't lying to you."

Carol was still mad at Steve for inventing a debate team field trip (in fact he had invented the whole debate team) so he could go on an out-of-town investigation for a few days. He'd been caught. And then grounded. And even though Steve wasn't grounded anymore, the incident had obviously created some lingering trust issues.

"Well, I wasn't lying, right?"

"Mmm."

"I mean, I closed the detective agency anyway."

"Surprise," Rick muttered.

"Well, I can only hope it stays closed," Carol said.

Rick laughed at something on the TV. The sound was still off, but the screen showed a small dog being lifted up by a vacuum cleaner attachment. Carol sat next to Rick on the couch and blocked his view of the television. Rick sighed and turned to join the conversation.

"I've never even heard of Model UN," Carol said. "Have you, Rick?"

Rick was leaning back to catch the end of the commercial. Now the vacuum cleaner had picked up a cat, and the dog from earlier had a paw over his face to indicate his dismay. "What?" Rick said, caught off guard.

"Model UN. Have you heard of it?"

"No. What is it? Like a hobby kit thing? UN? Model submarines?" Rick worked himself into a small panic proving his commitment to the conversation.

"Model *United Nations*," Steve said. Steve hadn't heard of it either until about a month ago, when his favorite teacher, Ms. Gilfeather, had left the school abruptly and been replaced by Mr. Meyer. Mr. Meyer had come out of retirement to finish out the school year, and on his first day he'd told the class, "When I taught seventh grade, we did Model UN every year— every single year—and even though it appears that *some* people didn't think Model UN was vital, and by the way we've seen where those people end up (here Mr. Meyer was clearly talking about Ms. Gilfeather), I'll be darned if I'm going to break my perfect record. Long story short, and this is good news for you, kids, I made some phone calls and pulled some strings, and we're going to work hard and put together a delegation for this year's Model UN in San Diego!" He'd delivered this last line like he expected the class to break into cheers, but nobody knew what he was talking about.

One month later and people still didn't know what Mr. Meyer was talking about. Steve had no idea what Model UN was—only that his class was representing Iceland (which didn't seem like a very powerful country; Mr. Meyer was clearly disappointed when he announced it, and mumbled something about "coming into the game late" and "getting last pick"), that they were going to San Diego for two nights, and that they'd spend the day in a hotel ballroom, listening to a lot of speeches and voting on stuff. The only one who seemed to have a real grasp of things was Dana, whom Mr. Meyer had chosen to give a presentation on cod fishing.

"Oh, Model United Nations," Rick said. "What's that?"

"It's too complicated to explain right now," Steve said.

"Well, Mr. Meyer talked my ear off for a half hour at work today. He kept bugging me about needing parent chaperones, and I kept explaining to him that some parents have to work and can't just take off to San Diego for three days. And in fact they also don't have time to listen to an old man talk about Model United Nations for an hour and a half in the middle of the day."

"Don't worry about it, Mom." Carol had developed a lot of guilt about never being able to go on field trips.

"When's the big trip?" Rick asked.

"Next week. We leave Thursday and come back Saturday."

Rick tugged on his blond mustache and smiled. "I'll do it."

"Do what?" Steve asked.

"I'll be a parent chaperone."

Steve straightened. "You can't."

"Why not?"

"Because parent chaperones have to be parents."

"Steve," Carol said.

"Well, then, I'll just be a chaperone. I've got three days off. It works out perfectly."

This was not working out perfectly.

"Great!" Carol said. She was clearly pleased with the idea. "I'll call Mr. Meyer tomorrow. Seriously, he would not stop talking today about needing parent chaperones."

Chaperone, Steve thought. Rick was just a chaperone, and preferably not even that.

"This will be fun!" Rick said. He pumped his fist in the air. "San Diego, here we come! Woo-woo! Model United Nations or bust!"

It was now official: Steve was not looking forward to this field trip. What he didn't know now was that he would never make it to the Model UN.

CHAPTER VIII

503 IN PROGRESS

THE NEXT THURSDAY Rick, Dana, and Steve sat shoulder to shoulder on the bench seat of Rick's truck. Rick, dressed in his "civilian clothes"—jeans, a navy Ocean Park Police Department T-shirt, and a navy Ocean Park Police Department baseball hat—tapped the steering wheel to a smooth jazz tune. Steve was eating his breakfast—dry cereal in a ziplock bag.

"That's no breakfast," Rick said, taking his eyes off the road for a second to shake his head at Steve.

Steve shrugged. "I like it."

"Breakfast is the most important meal of the day," Rick said.

"Really? I hadn't heard that before." Steve put

another handful of cereal in his mouth. Dana disguised his laugh as a yawn.

Rick was driving Steve and Dana to the train station (it had been too short notice, Mr. Meyer had sullenly announced last week, to get buses from the district). San Diego was a seven-hour journey down the coast, and the train was the only part of this fiasco Steve was looking forward to. Lots of the best Bailey Brothers books, including Bailey Brothers #31: *The Ghost Train Mystery* and #17: *All Aboard for Danger*, were set on trains. Steve had always wanted to take a long trip on a locomotive.

"Now, what's your girlfriend's name, Dana?" Rick asked, and waggled his eyebrows.

"Dana."

"Wait. Her name is Dana too?"

"Yep."

"Hmm." Rick narrowed his eyes.

Luckily, Rick's truck sat only three, or Other Dana would have surely been tagging along. In the school parking lot that morning Dana and his girlfriend had made plans to sit together on the train.

Rick turned to the boys. "And so when are you going to get a girlfriend, eh, Stevie?" More eyebrow waggling.

"No comment," Steve said. He'd been thinking about this a lot lately, and given the romantic entanglements of his two favorite people—his mom and Dana—Steve wasn't sure he ever wanted a girlfriend.

"Man, I remember when I was your guys's age, I probably had like ten girlfriends. There was this one girl, Holly Larson—"

Rick slammed on the brakes.

Steve and Dana were thrown forward.

"What do we have here?" Rick murmured. "A little five-oh-three in progress?"

"What's a five-oh-three?" Dana asked.

"Auto theft," Steve said. A few yards ahead, in front of the Ocean Park Pawn Shop, a man was working a wire hanger down the driver-side window of a late-model Honda Accord.

Rick pulled a portable police light out from behind the bench seat. He reached out the window and stuck it on the roof of his truck. A siren blared and a red strobe flashed. The man looked up and dropped the hanger. He looked worried.

"Is the siren really necessary?" Steve asked. "The guy is right there."

"I'm announcing the presence of a peace officer on the scene."

"I thought those things were only for undercover cops."

Rick looked defensive. "Wrong. You're wrong there. *Primarily used* by undercover police, maybe, but protocol allows a portable siren's use in any police emergency."

Rick slowly rolled his truck forward and double-parked next to the Accord.

"Most stolen car in America," Rick said, shaking his head.

"Unless the guy locked his keys in the car," Steve said.

"In front of the pawn shop?" Rick said. "Don't be naive, Steve. Store like that attracts a criminal element."

"It's seven thirty-five a.m. The store's not even open yet."

"Why don't we see what the investigation yields?"

"Guys," said Dana. "Can't you call for backup? Shouldn't we be getting to the train station?"

"Duty calls," Rick said, and hopped out of the truck. Steve slid out after him.

CHAPTER IX

A SLEUTHING TRICK

"Sir, Sergeant Rick Elliot, Ocean Park Police. Please take a few steps back from the vehicle." The police light continued to blast red flashes in the gray morning light. The man, dressed in black jeans and a blue button-down shirt, exhaled through his nose and muttered something Steve couldn't make out.

"Sir, care to tell me what's going on here?" Rick asked.

The man was matter-of-fact. "I locked my keys in the car."

Steve gave a victorious look at Rick, who smirked

and rolled his eyes. "So you're telling me that this is your vehicle."

"It's my car, yeah."

"What's your name, sir?"

"Cory Forsyth."

"And Mr. Forsyth, can you show me some identification and the vehicle's registration?"

"Well, my registration is in the car, obviously, and my wallet is in my coat pocket, right next to my keys. Which are in the car."

"Sir, please lower your voice."

"Look, I'm running late this morning—"

"So are we," Dana said softly out his open window.

"—and if I was stealing, I wouldn't use a wire hanger."

Rick's eyes flashed. "What would you use to steal a car, Mr. Forsyth?"

"I don't know! I'm a dental hygienist."

"And where does a dental hygienist get a hanger at seven thirty-five a.m.?"

"Probably that Laundromat," Steve said, pointing across the street.

"Yeah," said Cory.

"Stay out of this, Steve," said Rick.

While the man and Rick continued talking, Steve walked over to the sidewalk and looked in the pawn shop's window. It was his favorite window in Ocean Park: A selection of the store's wares—tubas, wristwatches, and various power tools—was scattered at the feet of a huge stuffed polar bear rearing up on its hind legs. The bear's name was Rex (there was a wooden sign around his neck), he'd been guarding the window for fifty years (pawned by a crazy hunter strapped for cash), and he was not for sale (Steve had asked). Among the merchandise strewn beneath Rex was a large magnifying glass with a wooden handle. Steve stared at it. The pawn shop was where Steve had purchased most of the equipment for his now-defunct crime lab, which still took up half his bedroom.

Steve turned back and examined the Accord.

"I'm just wondering," Rick was saying loudly, "how you, Cory Forsyth, a dental hygienist, know so much about what would or wouldn't make a good tool for breaking into a car."

"This is ridiculous!"

"Sir, I'm going to have to—"

"Excuse me," Steve interrupted. "You say this is your car, right?"

The man turned, exasperated. "Yes."

"Then can you tell me where you got this big scratch on the passenger door?"

The man's eyes widened. "What? It got scratched?"

Cory Forsyth ran over to the sidewalk and looked at the car's door. "What scratch?"

Steve smiled. He looked at Rick. "This is his car."

"How do you know?"

"Because there is no scratch. Think about it: If he was lying about owning the car, he would have made up a story when I asked him about the scratch—he'd have no way of know that I was lying too. But instead he freaked out about his car being damaged."

Mr. Forsyth put his hands on his hips and nodded. "See?"

"Oh, come on," Rick said.

"You know I'm right," said Steve.

Rick didn't say anything, but he turned back to his truck.

"Guys," said Dana. "We only have thirteen minutes to make the train."

CHAPTER X

COLLISION COURSE!

"WE'RE GOING TO MISS THE TRAIN." Dana, distressed, eyed the dash clock.

They were all three back in the truck and speeding through downtown Ocean Park.

The Sunset Coastliner for San Diego was scheduled to leave the station in Santa Lucia at 8:15. It was now 8:02. Santa Lucia was fifteen minutes away with no traffic.

There was traffic.

"We're going to miss the train," Dana repeated.

"Oh, no we aren't," Rick said. Grinning, he put the police light back on top of the car. "Here we go." The truck lurched forward.

"And how is this a police emergency?" Steve asked.

"Weird that the famous private detective has suddenly become a stickler for police protocol," Rick said as they passed a car.

"I'm not a private detective anymore," Steve said.

"Never were." Rick snorted, keeping his eyes on the road.

"What do you call what Steve did back there?" Dana said, looking up from the clock. "That was some pretty good detective work."

"Wasn't detective work," Rick said. Steve wouldn't have called it detective work either, because he wasn't a detective anymore, but he didn't like it when Rick said it.

"Then what would you call it, Rick?" Dana asked.

"Reckless. Cheap. Stunt work."

"It worked, didn't it?" Steve said.

"We'll see," Rick said. Rick had called the station to dispatch an officer to the pawn shop before they'd left the scene, but it was pretty clear he was just saving face.

Dana turned to Steve. "Where'd you learn that trick? Asking him about the scratch? Was that from the Bailey Brothers?"

"No. It just kind of came to me." Dana smiled and nodded. Steve leaned back. It had felt good out there, solving a mystery before breakfast. *Or mid-breakfast,* he thought, putting another handful of cereal in his mouth. And he hadn't even been solving a mystery so much as asking a couple questions. Nothing an ordinary citizen couldn't—or shouldn't, for that matter—do to clear an innocent man's name.

"Come on, come on," Rick said through gritted teeth. He honked his horn at an old van that was moving slowly. "Pull over. Pull over."

"What do we do if we miss the train?" Steve asked. Dana grimaced.

"Not an issue," Rick said. "Not an issue. We're making the train." Rick swung into the opposite lane to pass the van.

A black Suburban was coming toward them, fast.

CHAPTER XI

RACING TO THE STATION

THE HORNS OF THE TWO VEHICLES competed loudly for a few slow seconds. Steve cringed in his seat as the SUV hurtled toward them. Rick braked and swerved back into his lane behind the van as the Suburban flew by, its continuous honk distorting into a whine and then a bellow as it passed.

Steve was sandwiched between Dana and the window. Everyone in the car collected himself. The van in front of them had pulled over to the right-hand side.

"Now he gets it," Rick said, accelerating gently.

"Could you try not to kill us, Rick?" Steve said. His face was hot, and his heart beat quickly. "I know you're earning big points with my mom for this chaperone thing, but she'd be pretty mad if you killed us."

"I avoided the crash, didn't I? You have to admit that was pretty good defensive driving." Rick's face was flushed.

"Yeah, after the offensive driving."

"We are going to miss this train," Dana said.

"Man, chill out," Rick said. He was driving fast again, but a little more carefully. "We're going to make it."

"Look at the clock."

It was 8:09.

"You're obsessing with that thing." Rick reached over with his right hand and jammed the buttons on the clock until its face read 12:47. "Trust me. Now you're on Rick time."

Dana sighed.

They sped down South Street into Santa Lucia. "Grab your stuff, guys. We're making a left in three blocks and we're at the station. We'll run onto that train just as they're saying 'all aboard.'" Dana strapped his backpack over one shoulder. Steve put his suitcase in his lap. The suitcase had been his grandfather's, and Steve's mom had let him take it on the trip. It was brown and trimmed with tan leather, and it seemed perfectly suited for train travel, although perhaps unwieldy for sprinting. Steve began dreading the run.

He didn't need to worry. No sooner had the sign for Railroad Avenue become legible than a bell began clanging. A red and white barrier lowered and blocked the road.

Rick braked and swore. "You've got to be kidding."

The engine's whistle rattled the truck, and the train rolled slowly through the intersection. Car after shiny car, the sides lined like sneakers with red, white, and blue stripes, passed in front of them. For a while nobody said anything. They just sat and watched.

"We missed the train," Dana said.

The flashing red of Rick's roof-mounted portable police light was reflected in the cars' shiny metal exterior.

"What do we do now?" Rick said.

"Well," said Steve, "you've got that nifty siren. Why don't you just pull the train over?"

CHAPTER XII

A CURIOUS OCCURRENCE

FOUR HOURS LATER Steve, Dana, and Rick stood on platform 2 of Santa Lucia Station, waiting to board the next train for San Diego. Over a tense lunch at a nearby taquería, Rick had announced his new plan: They would meet up with the class tonight at the hotel and have a full day of Model UN tomorrow just like everyone else, so really it didn't matter that they'd missed the train, and in fact this new plan was probably even a better plan, because why were they booked on such an early train in the first place?

It was fun seeing Rick fret, and now they'd get to ride down without Other Dana, so Steve was in good spirits as the train pulled up to the station.

Their train stopped at the platform and waited, emitting a dull diesel hum, but the doors stayed closed.

"When do we get on?" Dana asked.

"I don't know," Rick said. "I don't really ride trains."

"Probably the stationmaster has to say 'all aboard' first," Steve said, looking around for a stationmaster. He didn't see one, or anyone who looked like they worked for the railroad, on the platform. (And really, the man who'd sold them their tickets at the station, a man who obviously worked for the railroad, hadn't really looked like he worked for the railroad: He wore no cap or coat, just khakis and a mustard-stained short-sleeved shirt.)

A faint female voice came from a megaphone mounted on the roof of the platform's shelter: "Passengers for the twelve forty-five Sunset Coastliner for San Diego are requested to please wait at the platform for a brief ten-minute delay. We apologize for the inconvenience."

"Oh, you're kidding," Rick said.

Steve put down his suitcase.

"What do you think is happening?" Dana asked.

Nobody answered.

Steve watched as three cops in uniform emerged from the station and crossed to the platform. One hopped up into the engine. A few seconds later the door on the first car opened, and another officer entered the train. The third stood on the platform and watched the assembled passengers waiting to board.

Rick followed Steve's eye line and saw the cops. "Good," he said. "Wait here. I'll figure out what's going on." He strode over to the officer. After they exchanged a few sentences and shook hands, Rick returned to where the boys were standing. He nodded confidently. "He said it will only be about ten minutes."

"Well, we learned that from the megaphone," Steve said, pointing to the ceiling.

"Did he say why the police were here?" Dana asked.

Rick shrugged sharply. "Routine. Just . . . routine."

"Seems weird," Dana said, and looked at Steve skeptically.

A familiar tingle spread in Steve's stomach. There was something going on here. He looked down at the policeman waiting by the engine. The officer was wary, watchful. He was looking for something or someone. There was a mystery in progress right over there. Steve was sure of it. His brain began whirring. Steve shuddered. No. He was done sleuthing. Retired. Out of the game for good.

Steve needed to distract himself, to quiet his mind. He turned and started walking—away from the front of the train, away from whatever was going on with the police.

But if Steve wanted to walk away from danger, he was walking in the wrong direction.

CHAPTER XIII

THE PHANTOM CAR

THE SUNSET COASTLINER had an engine and seven cars, and each car's side bore the name of a California landmark. The one in front of Steve was SAN SIMEON BAY, its name painted on the metal in deep blue. Steve decided to distract himself by seeing whether any of the cars was named after Ocean Park.

Next up was VENICE BEACH. Whatever was going on really wasn't any of Steve's business. BODEGA BAY. Although Steve's mom was always saying that if a person got hurt in front of her, she had a responsibility to help them, because she was a nurse: She was always sort of on the job. MOUNT BALDY. But it was different for detectives, right? A detective didn't have an obligation to solve every mystery that came his way. DEATH VALLEY. And anyway, Steve wasn't a detective anymore. He was a kid. (An air conditioner hissed and startled him.) Yes, he wanted nothing to do with any of this.

Steve stopped at the last car.

It had no name.

That was weird. He looked at the preceding car. Next to the words DEATH VALLEY was a number: 8802. He ran back to MOUNT BALDY. 8008. BODEGA BAY was 8083. But when he walked back to the last car, the nameless car, Steve saw that its number was 724. Three digits. That was odd too. He took a step back. The car looked just like the other cars—silver and striped—but the windows that lined its side weren't windows at all. They were metal, too, and when he examined one, he found his own confused face staring back at him.

Because he was looking at his reflection, Steve was able to see the man with the long scar come up behind him.

Steve felt the menacing gaze of the scar-faced man.

CHAPTER XIV

AN UNPLEASANT ENCOUNTER

"See something interesting?"

Steve turned around and faced the man. The man's face was long and thin, marred by the scar on his cheek and a nose that had been broken more than once. And though his face was fearsome, and he wore a sneer, his tone was sharp but not unkind.

Steve shrugged and started back toward Rick and Dana, who were watching him from down the platform.

"Hey!" the man shouted. "I asked you a question." His tone was now unkind.

Steve turned back around, even though he didn't want to.

"I said," the man said slowly, "see something interesting?" He pronounced every syllable of the last word.

Steve had no reason to lie to the man. He was just a kid looking at a train. "This car doesn't have a name on it."

"So?"

"Well, all the other cars have names."

"So?"

"So that's kind of interesting. You asked if I had seen anything interesting."

"And why," the man asked, "is that interesting?"

Steve was getting tired of this. "Look. I don't know. It just seemed a little weird. You know, that the last car didn't have a name. Or windows. That's all."

The man raised his eyebrows. "Maybe that's because it's a caboose."

Steve laughed. "Freight trains have cabooses. Not passenger trains."

Now he squinted. "You some kind of train enthusiast?"

"No."

"Just a snoop, then." The man put his hands on his hips and looked Steve up and down. He took a long time doing it, making a big show, as if to demonstrate to Steve that he was taking everything in, and that he didn't like what he saw. Steve took the opportunity to get a good look at the man, too. He was tall and reedy, wearing shabby gray pants and a brown tweed coat. His white shirt was wrinkled and a little bit yellowed. And then, underneath the man's blazer, in the space created by the man's akimbo arms, Steve saw something truly interesting: a holstered pistol.

CHAPTER XV

ALL ABOARD!

THE MAN NOTICED Steve notice the gun. He dropped his arms. His face was uncertain.

A bell sounded pleasantly, and the doors on every car but the last whooshed open. The megaphone creaked: "Attention now boarding the twelve forty-five Sunset Coastliner to San Diego thank you for your patience now boarding the twelve forty-five Sunset Coastliner to San Diego all aboard." That was it: "all aboard" attached unceremoniously to the end of a rushed announcement. No stationmaster. No whistle or bell. Steve wasn't so alarmed by the man's pistol that he didn't have room to feel a little disappointed.

And really, the gun was none of his business. He nodded curtly to the man, ran to Rick and Dana, picked up his suitcase, and boarded the train. And even though Steve planned to mind his own business, he hoped the man with the gun stayed at the station.

CHAPTER XVI

AMBUSH AT TURRIS SENEX

ALTHOUGH STEVE HAD BEEN TRYING not to think about the Bailey Brothers books all week, he couldn't get them out of his head as he boarded the train. In the Bailey Brothers books, trains were often hijacked, usually filled with criminals (or sometimes with defecting nuclear scientists), and, at least once, driven by a hypnotized engineer. But they were always elegant ways to travel. See, for example, their first trip down the rails in *All Aboard for Danger*:

"These sure are swell digs!" Shawn grinned, approvingly surveying their drawing room. Fresh towels lay folded next to the sink, three pairs of fluffy slippers sat on a fine rug, and a deck of playing cards lay on the reading table.

"Anyone up for a game of Go Fish?" Kevin queried.

"Maybe after a nap," mumbled Shawn, who was still knackered from the previous night's stakeout of the old paint factory.

"And I'm going to check out the dining car," Ernest announced. "I hear they have a terrific charcoal-broiled sirloin steak with maître d'hôtel butter. And a delicious chocolate sundae."

"Just remember," Kevin teased, winking at his stout chum, "there are other people on this train who need to eat, and the kitchen doesn't restock until Cleveland!" The boys all laughed.

Shawn, who had the top bunk at the Bailey residence, yawned and lowered the pull-down bed.

Ba-ang! Shawn flew backward onto the floor. The smell of gunpowder overpowered the compartment.

"Nattering nanny goats! That was a

close call!" Shawn exclaimed. He pointed to a sawed-off shotgun mounted high on the wall. "I triggered that booby trap when I lowered the bed!"

"Zounds!" cried Kevin. "You almost took more than a nap."

"Well," riposted Shawn, clambering up to bed, "the shotgun may be a bit unwelcoming, but the mattress sure is top-notch!"

The 12:45 Sunset Coastliner to San Diego was not top-notch.

The train in Steve's mind was all brass and wood and wool; the train Steve was in was polyester and plastic and Naugahyde.

Where were the doors that slid open to spacious sleepers? Where was the club car? Where were the porters with their flat caps and brass buttons?

The car was just one open room filled with rows of seats—two on each side with an aisle running down the middle. The carpet was grease-stained and gum-pocked. Most windows bore greasy palm prints.

"Don't we have a compartment?" Steve asked, looking at his ticket.

Rick scoffed. "I don't think they have compartments

in these trains, Stevie. This isn't one of your Bailey Boys books."

"Bailey *Brothers*," Steve said.

"Exactly," said Rick. "Take a seat."

Steve walked by a man reading a paperback and a bored-looking teenager. He passed a man and woman who had a small child and three half-eaten sandwiches on their laps. Their hands were all orange with Cheetos dust. Why weren't these people eating in the dining car? Steve wondered. He followed Dana into a row. The worn fabric on their chairs was covered in blue, turquoise, and yellow rectangles—it looked like a pixelated photograph of the ocean, and Steve found the pattern unsettling. He considered asking Dana for the window seat, so he could look at the actual ocean, but his friend had been in a bad mood since they missed the train that morning.

Rick sat across the aisle from the boys. He put his duffel on the empty seat next to him and took out two knitting needles and some skeins of yarn.

"I'm making a pair of camping socks," Rick said when he noticed Steve watching him.

"Cool," Steve replied.

"It *is* cool," Rick said, and started knitting. "If you think it's weird for a guy to knit—"

"I didn't say anything," Steve said.

"—then you have been sleeping under a rock or something, because men's knitting circles are all over the news."

"The news?"

"Yes. The news." Rick started knitting.

Meanwhile Dana had taken a thick book out of his backpack. Steve was horrified when he saw its cover:

Steve couldn't believe anyone was comfortable holding that thing in public. Steve felt awkward just sitting next to it.

"Seriously?" Steve asked. "I'm bored. You're just going to read?"

"Not the whole time. We've got a seven-hour trip. I just want to get past this part. It's really good. Didn't you bring a book?"

Steve's face flushed. He didn't answer. Steve and Dana used to hang out and read a lot—and Steve would always be reading the Bailey Brothers.

Dana opened to a bookmarked page. Steve looked over his friend's shoulder:

VII

Transportation spells always nauseated Kallendar, but he tried to hide his queasiness from Brynwyllyn, who did not seem at all affected by their journey. She studied him for a moment, her cornflower-blue eyes quizzical and surprisingly wise, and Kallendar immediately realized the futility of hiding his condition from an elven healer.

"Do you need a few minutes to rest, mage?" she asked blankly.

Her indifference stung him. "No," he said, standing. As he rose, he cursed himself for taking his last cysurberry yesterday as treatment for the small headache the anifornum had caused him. If he was to make it to Nzorl-Ut, he reminded himself, he would have to use his magick rations more carefully. "Let us continue," Kallendar said bravely. "We are running out of time."

The two figures began down the pebbly shore in the misty dawn. Ahead of them stood a graying tower alone on the sea. Kallendar's heart rose as he eyed the ancient stone structure. Turris Senex. Somewhere within slumbered the Book of Krunum-Krog.

An albatross circled and let out a mournful cry as they approached the tower. Snorri cawed loudly in response, and Kallendar reached to his left shoulder and ruffled his familiar's inky feathers.

"I think Snorri has found love at first sight."

Brynwyllyn laughed. Her smile warmed Kallendar's heart, and he fought to keep his mind on the task ahead.

The runes on the wall of Turris Senex were surprisingly easy to decipher. But when Kallendar and Brynwyllyn stepped through the portal in the smooth stone, the entrance closed, sealing them inside, in darkness. Kallendar incanted a simple illumination spell, but nothing happened. "Maybe we're too close to the water," he muttered unsurely. He pulled his athame from his baldric. The blade glowed light blue, faintly illuminating a twisting hall leading into the tower's bowels.

"Well, at least we've got some light," Brynwyllyn said. "Come on." She started down the path.

The hallway wound upward, and soon Kallendar was consumed by doubts. What if he was wrong, and the Book was not here? After all, he was just a masterless apprentice who got magick-sickness from casting even a simple dissumulo enchantment. He considered returning home to the farm in Cristolin, tending to the goats, becoming Kallendar the Yeoman again. He imagined his Uncle Kaldrick's sneer when he saw Kallendar walk up the garden path. No. He could never go back.

Kallendar stopped. His athame no longer glowed blue: It was red. "Brynwyllyn," he whispered fiercely. "Danger."

There was a low groan from deep within the tower.

Brynwyllyn sniffed the stale air. Her face grew grave with concern. "Balrogs." Suddenly a chill descended in the hall. A shriek pierced the air. Kallendar turned to run and found that the way back was blocked by a wall of smooth black stone.

"We're trapped!"

He spun around to find two shadow demons, their ghoulish faces surrounded by halos of icy blue flame. They pointed their bony fingers forward. Brynwyllyn recited a basic dryad protection spell that Kallendar knew would be futile against these grim foes. It was hopeless: They were barrow bound.

Kallendar tossed Brynwyllyn his athame. She was more adept with the blade anyway; she'd proven that at Tongullin Fields. Kallendar's hand went instinctively to his father's rusty blade. "Ouch!" The weapon's pommel was searing hot. He unsheathed the sword— its edge glowed green. Could it be? Of course! The old broadsword he'd inherited—the one Kaldrick had sneeringly called junk—was Tyrfing, the dwarvish blade blessed with boggart magick, forged in the caverns of Longurdl by Untril the Red Smith, son of Brindi the

Impossible, son of Arnuldr the Unfortunate, son of Karl the . . ."

"Oh, come on," Steve said.

Dana looked up. "What?"

"This book is ridiculous. Those baldrics were about to attack—"

"Balrogs."

"What's the difference?"

"A baldric is a belt worn around a tunic. A balrog is a demon."

"Whatever. The demons were attacking, and then all of a sudden the story turns into a sword's family tree."

"Once you get into it, the genealogy stuff is actually really exciting."

"I can't believe you just said that." Steve looked out the window at the sunlight bouncing off the Pacific. "Let me ask you something. How big is this Brynwyllyn?"

"What?"

"The elf. Like, is she Keebler-sized, or human-sized?"

"Human-sized."

"Yeah, I don't get that," Steve said.

"Hmm," Dana said, and continued reading.

Steve had trouble settling. He pulled the magazine

from his seat pocket, but the crossword was already filled out. So was Dana's. He slumped in his chair.

What was this train doing with a nameless car? It wouldn't be so strange if it hadn't been for the scar-faced man hanging out back there with a handgun. A handgun Steve wasn't supposed to see. You could call it a coincidence, and coincidences were the last refuge of the lazy detective. And Steve was not lazy. Of course, he was also not a detective.

Steve's thinking was interrupted by the arrival of the conductor.

"Tickets." This guy at least looked the part, white-haired and friendly, dressed in a neatly pressed uniform. It gave Steve hope that they were just in a dumpy car, and that the nice parts of the train were somewhere else.

"Excuse me," he said, handing his ticket over, "where's the dining car?"

The conductor made two sharp clicks with his silver hole punch, then pointed to the front of the train. "First car. Up past business class." Good. Away from the "caboose."

"Can I go?" Steve asked Rick.

"Sure." Rick put down his knitting needles and reached in his pocket. "Here." He handed Steve a five-dollar bill.

"Thanks." That was nice. Steve didn't like it when Rick was nice. And he definitely didn't like taking other people's money, either. Steve had made five thousand dollars off a single case as a private detective, but his mom had made him put it away for college. And he doubted five bucks would go far in the dining car. Those places were swanky: white tablecloths and fancy china. It probably wouldn't buy a chocolate sundae, let alone charcoal-broiled sirloin steak with maître d'hôtel butter.

"Want to come?" Steve asked Dana.

"Maybe when I get to the end of this chapter."

"Okay."

The second Steve rose, there was a loud roar. The whole car shook.

CHAPTER XVII

MEET CLAIRE MARRINER

THERE WAS A SHOCKING FLASH of metal as an oncoming train passed theirs on the left. Steve stumbled, startled.

Rick chuckled. "Still need to get your train legs, eh, Stevie?"

Steve frowned. "What?"

"Train legs. Like sea legs, for trains."

Dana looked up from his book. "I don't think that's a thing, Rick."

Steve smiled. Now *that* was the old Dana.

He headed for the front of the train.

Steve hoped business class would be better, but it wasn't. As far as Steve could tell, the only difference between business class and coach class was that the stains on the business-class carpets were left by businessmen. (The very fact that Steve was allowed to walk through business class on his way to the dining car told him it wasn't a very exclusive way to travel.)

Man, train travel has really gone downhill, Steve thought as he walked past a snoring man in a gray suit. Still, he looked forward to sitting at a table, sipping celery juice or hot chocolate and watching the Pacific Ocean go by.

But the dining car wasn't even called the dining car. It was called the café car, and it was about as glamorous as the snack bar at a junior varsity volleyball game. The whole place smelled like burned coffee and bad soup.

A man sat behind a counter, surrounded by snacks. He wore a light beard and a loose-fitting apron, and he looked at Steve without much interest. Behind him was a microwave, cups of breakfast cereals and dehydrated ramen, candy bars, bags of chips, and bottles ranging in size from tiny to just normal. The lighting was harshly fluorescent and completely unnecessary in the daytime, and it made Steve's mood even worse. All the plasticky tables and chairs were empty except one.

A girl about Steve's age was drinking a cup of something hot and reading a book.

The girl had long brown hair and light freckles and glasses. She rested her chin on both hands and held the book open with her elbows. When she reached for her cup, she didn't even look up or take her elbow from the page open in front of her.

She looked nice.

That was ridiculous. Steve didn't know anything about her. She was just a girl reading a book.

Steve wondered what she was reading. He thought about asking her. In his mind she was reading a Bailey Brothers book (even though it was paperback and so couldn't be a Bailey Brothers book). And then Steve could tell her that he'd read that one. And she'd be impressed, and they'd talk about their favorite Bailey Brothers mysteries and maybe even Steve's own adventures as a detective.

"Holler if you want anything," the man behind the counter said to Steve.

The girl looked up, and Steve quickly looked at the man. "I'm just looking," he said quickly. The man smiled and nodded.

Steve looked at the girl.

The girl looked at Steve.

Steve looked away.

The girl read while the view sped by.

Steve felt queasy. He studied a nearby poster advertising the UTZ FAMILY OF SNACKS while he organized his thoughts. Should he go up and talk to her? She was his age, and they were both on the train, so why not? But it wasn't like he needed to make friends or anything. Dana was here. Staring at a photograph of some pretzels, Steve decided to leave the car.

"See anything interesting?" a voice behind him asked. Steve turned. It was the girl. She was at least six inches taller than he was.

"You're the second person to ask me that today."

"What a coincidence," she said.

Steve usually didn't believe in coincidences, but he was grateful for this one. It seemed like a good omen.

"I'm Claire Marriner," she said.

"Oh. I'm Steve Brixton," said Steve. "What are you doing on this train?" The question came out too harshly and left an unpleasant aftertaste in Steve's mouth.

"I'm taking a trip with my uncle."

Steve nodded. "Cool. Cool."

"How about you?"

Steve had to think a bit before he remembered. "I'm going to this Model UN thing in San Diego."

"Oh."

Steve didn't know why, but after an agonizing

silence he said, "Yeah, I used to be a private detective. Now I'm retired."

Claire looked at him. "That doesn't even make sense."

"Yes it does."

"How old are you?"

"Twelve."

"Me too. You're too young to be a detective, let alone a *retired* detective."

"That's ridiculous. I was a detective. My picture was in the newspaper and everything."

Claire didn't say anything. She just smiled dismissively. This infuriated Steve.

"I was," he said.

"Okay," she said brightly.

"What do you know about sleuthing?"

"My uncle's a private detective."

Well. This was unexpected.

"What's his name?"

"Cy Marriner."

Steve crossed his arms. "Well, I've never heard of him."

"You're not supposed to have heard of him. That's why they call them *private* detectives," Claire said.

"No it's not."

"What?"

"They call them private detectives because they don't work for—"

"I know, I know," Claire said impatiently, "but still, it would be hard to work undercover if your picture was in the paper."

Steve shrugged. He'd never had any trouble working undercover.

"Anyway, I better go back to my seat. My uncle's probably wondering where I am."

"Where are you sitting?"

"Oh, back a few cars. I don't know the seat number or anything. These cars all look exactly the same." She laughed.

"Yeah!" Steve agreed, probably too enthusiastically.

"Well, maybe I'll see you later, old man," Claire said.

"What?" Steve said, but she was already gone.

It took Steve a couple seconds to realize that "old man" had been a joke about his retirement. He didn't like the joke. In fact pretty much all of his conversation with Claire Marriner had been irritating, and Steve wondered why he'd asked where she was sitting. He decided he'd rather not see Claire Marriner again.

When Steve turned around, he noticed that Claire had left her book facedown on the table. He went over and picked it up. It was bound in green cloth and embossed with an *A* on the cover. The title on the spine was *Pride and Prejudice*. He saved her page, using a napkin as a bookmark. Obviously, Steve decided, she would need her book back. It was his duty to return it.

He was looking forward to seeing Claire Marriner again.

CHAPTER XVIII

THE GIRL VANISHES

BOOK IN HAND, Steve exited the café car. Grabbing unoccupied seat backs to keep his balance, Steve looked around for Claire in business class. He didn't think she'd be in this car, and she wasn't—it was just a bunch of men and women, most of them in drab suits, reading magazines and talking quietly. Claire wasn't in Steve's car either, although Steve already knew that. Dana was still deep in Wizards' Worlds, and Rick was napping, slack-jawed, his head leaning against the window.

Steve walked by quietly. When he passed the

family, the man was holding the little girl up so she could look out the window. There were orange handprints all over the front of his T-shirt. The girl had her face pressed right up against the glass. She squealed. Her mother laughed. Steve looked back to make sure Rick was still asleep, and so he bumped right into someone coming toward him.

"Sorry," Steve said, turning.

It was the scar-faced man.

"You again?" The man looked disgusted.

"I said sorry," said Steve, and hurried to the next car.

Claire was not here.

Nor was she in the next car.

Or the car after that.

In fact, besides Dana there were no other kids on the train, let alone a girl with light freckles and long brown hair.

Steve stood at the front of the train's fifth car, the one called DEATH VALLEY, he remembered. There was only one car left: the phantom car. Steve swallowed hard. He continued down the aisle.

The window on the door at the back of the car was almost completely covered by a bright orange sticker. It said DANGER—NO ENTRY—HIGH VOLTAGE, and it had a picture of a stick figure getting zapped by two bolts of lightning. The bolts were hitting the figure's back and chest in a perfect, painful V, as if hurled by some angry and ambidextrous Greek god. Steve stopped and considered his next move.

"Can't go back there, son," came a voice from Steve's left. The white-haired conductor was sitting in the window seat, smiling. "Dangerous."

"What's back there?" Steve asked. "What's in that car?"

"Electrical stuff. Wiring. And some cargo."

Steve nodded. He was relieved to have solved the mystery of the phantom car.

But there was still the mystery of Claire Marriner. Steve looked again at the thick black lightning bolts and got woozy when he thought of Claire coming back here accidentally.

"Hey," Steve said, hiding his concern. "Have you seen a girl about my age come through this car? Maybe she came back through this door? In the last five minutes or so?"

"Sure haven't," the man said. "And I've been here for a quarter hour. Nobody goes back there—the sign stops 'em. Although"—he leaned over conspiratorially— "it's not all that dangerous. You can't even get into the last car from inside the train."

Steve's head was all swirling clouds. "Okay," he said. "Thanks."

"Good luck finding that girl," the conductor said, and winked.

Steve turned and hurried toward the front of the train.

CHAPTER XIX

A DESPERATE SEARCH

TRAIN LEGS OR NO, Steve almost ran down the train's center aisle. His heart and lungs were working fast. But his brain felt like it wasn't working at all. All his thoughts were flinging wildly about, then slapping against the inside of his skull. Claire Marriner had disappeared. How? It was impossible. And yet she was nowhere to be found.

Steve must have missed her on his way back through the train. That was the only reasonable explanation.

And so Steve began anxiously checking and double-checking the rows of seats. Whenever a passenger looked up at him, Steve quickly changed his expression from panicked to politely benign. But few people did notice Steve, which gave him plenty of time to examine them for false noses, concealed switchblades, or other indicators of criminal nature. There was something shady underway on this train— Steve had suspected as much since he saw the cops on the platform—and now Claire was caught up in it.

After a blur of faces—some exhausted, irritated, or wrinkled, but none particularly nefarious—Steve found himself back in the café car. The scar-faced man sat at a table, glowering at him while emptying a tiny plastic wine bottle into a big plastic cup.

Claire was not in the café car.

Steve, sweating, turned around and walked back through the train.

This time, at the back of each car Steve got on the floor in case Claire was hiding under a seat. Now people stared. Steve didn't care.

Why would a girl be hiding under a seat? Steve asked himself, his chin resting on the car's cool floor. (He was only dimly aware of the grease stains.) It didn't make sense.

But how could a girl disappear from a train?

A small, white dog barked at him from within its carrier.

He got up. The dog's owner looked at him disapprovingly. Obviously, this woman didn't understand, and neither did the dog.

Steve checked the train's bathrooms. Only one was occupied. Steve loitered outside the door. He knocked. There was no answer. He softly pounded his right fist in his left palm. The red tab by the door's handle clicked over to green. The handle turned. The door opened. A man with a shaved head and a striped scarf exited into the car.

"All yours," he said.

"Oh, I don't need it," Steve said.

The man raised his eyebrows and walked down the aisle. Steve followed close behind him. Why was this guy walking so slowly? The man gave Steve a strange look over his right shoulder.

"Can I help you?" he said.

"No," Steve replied, and took the opportunity to squeeze past him.

"Weird kid," Steve heard the man mutter as he hurried down the train. Steve's face flushed. At least Steve wasn't wearing a scarf inside a train—that was really weird. Like sunglasses at night, only not at all cool. Although maybe you get cold when you don't have any hair.

Soon Steve was back in the sixth car.

No Claire. He went only halfway back this time, smiled weakly at the conductor to eliminate any suspicion, and started walking forward again.

This was the last trip he would make.

He would find Claire this time.

He looked at the passengers as he went by. They listened to music, typed on laptops, and told stories. Steve looked sharply at a man who laughed loudly at some joke. He felt angry with these people, casually going about their business while a crisis unfolded on their train.

He stared at a woman reading a book. "Excuse me," he said. He tried to take the edge out of his voice. "Have you seen a girl about my age, with brown hair and glasses?" The woman shook her head and wrinkled her nose like Steve's question had smelled bad. She went back to her book.

Steve checked all the luggage racks for brown-haired stowaways.

Claire was not up there.

Claire was not anywhere.

Claire Marriner had disappeared.

CHAPTER XX

ENLISTING A CHUM

STEVE PLOPPED DOWN IN HIS SEAT. Rick was still slack-jawed and sleeping. Dana looked up from his book.

"Where have you been?" he asked.

Steve was breathing heavily. He brushed his hair back from his forehead. "I met this girl in the café car," Steve said.

"Oooooooohh," said Dana.

"No, listen. She disappeared," Steve said. And then added: "And also it's not even like that."

Dana's face got serious. "Disappeared?"

"Yeah. She just disappeared. I met her in the café car, and now she's not on the train."

"What are you talking about?"

Steve told Dana about Claire, about his search through the cars, about the conductor and the phantom car and the scar-faced man and the woman reading a book.

"Weird," said Dana.

"I know," said Steve.

"But that's impossible," said Dana.

"I know," said Steve. "Unless she's a wizard."

Dana ignored that. He hesitated, and then asked, "Are you sure there was a girl?"

"What?"

"I don't know," Dana said quickly. "It's just I'm trying to think of a rational explanation, and one rational explanation is that you like hallucinated this."

"That's a stupid explanation," Steve said. "I have her book." He opened *Pride and Prejudice* to the flyleaf. There, written in cursive with a ballpoint pen, was the name "Claire Marriner."

"She has nice handwriting," Dana said.

"Yeah," Steve said.

"Oh!" said Dana. "Maybe she's in one of the bathrooms!"

Steve rolled his eyes. "I checked the bathrooms. Come on, Dana. I'm a . . ."

Dana leaned forward. "You're a what?"

"I'm a retired detective, okay?"

Dana rubbed his chin. "So what's the plan? I mean, there's nothing we can do, right? Should we wake Rick up and tell him?"

Steve's wide-open mouth conveyed his sense of betrayal. "Him? Come on. How many times have I outsolved that guy?"

Dana shrugged.

"Look," said Steve, "there is an innocent person who is almost definitely in some kind of danger right now."

"Yeah, I know," Dana said.

Steve just nodded.

"So what are you saying?" Dana asked.

"What I'm saying is that I've been trying to stay out of the game—"

"The game?"

"Yes. I've been turning down jobs left and right. But I can't sit back and let this happen. This girl needs a detective. Her life may depend on it. I'm coming out of retirement for one last case. I'm reopening the Brixton Brothers Detective Agency."

"Okay."

"Dana, we're back in business."

CHAPTER XXI

BACK IN THE GAME

"We?"

"You're not going to help?"

Dana had never much liked sleuthing to begin with, and he liked it even less after being kidnapped twice (Dana said three times, but the third was really just an attempted kidnapping). And getting shot at in a pool. And in a forest.

"Someone's life could be on the line," Steve said.

Dana groaned. "Fine. I'll help. But we are not in business together."

"Good," said Steve. "Now here's the plan—"

"Wait," said Dana. "You said her uncle's a private detective, right? Let's get him to help."

"And go asking every man traveling alone if he's Cy Marriner? Wrong. That wastes valuable time. Plus I'm not sure she was telling the truth."

"Really?"

"Yeah, maybe she was trying to show me up. I mean, I've never heard of a private detective named Cy Marriner."

"But they're called *private* detectives."

"Yeah, but that's not why!" Steve composed himself. "Look, we don't need to find him, because I already know where Claire Marriner is."

"What?"

"I mean I think I know. Which is one definition of a hunch. And a hunch is basically as good as or better than knowing. Look, Shawn Bailey always says, 'Sherlock Holmes always says, "Rule out the impossible. What's left, however improbable, is the solution."'"

Steve took a worn black notebook from his back pocket. He showed Dana a page:

MYSTERY: WHERE IS CLAIRE MARRINER?

PLACE	IS CLAIRE MARRINER HERE?
Seat	No
Bathroom	No
Underneath a seat	No
Luggage rack	No

"Why would she be in the luggage rack?" Dana asked.

"I'm being really thorough, okay?"

"Okay. So where is she?"

Steve added to the list:

The Phantom Car

"Well we know she's not there," Dana said.

Steve smiled. "How?"

"Because the conductor said she didn't come by him. And that you couldn't get in the car from the train anyway."

"And why should we believe the conductor?"

"Why shouldn't we believe the conductor?"

"Because Shawn Bailey always says, 'Sherlock Holmes always—'"

"Okay, okay." Dana looked worried. "Are you sure she's in the phantom car?"

"No," Steve said. "But we have to check it with our own eyes before we can cross it off. We have to get past the conductor and into that car."

"And how are we going to do that?"

"We are going to climb on top of this train."

CHAPTER XXII

PLAN OF ACTION

"OH NO. THAT'S STUPID. THAT'S SO DUMB," Dana said, looking out the window. "We're not climbing on top of any trains."

"Sure we are."

Dana turned back to Steve. "People don't do that, Steve."

"Actually, detectives do it all the time," Steve said. "Check it out. I'll prove it."

Steve stood on his chair and pulled down his grandfather's suitcase. The brass clasps opened with sharp snaps. Steve opened the lid. Inside were clothes, a toiletry kit, and two bags of fruit snacks. Steve felt along the edge of the case. The lining came loose in the corner. Steve's hand disappeared in the space between the lining and the shell. He dug around for a few seconds and then pulled out a shiny red book. Two carefully groomed teens posed with a grateful policeman on its cover.

It was *The Bailey Brothers' Detective Handbook*.

Dana's eyes got big. "I thought you threw those books away!"

Steve shook his head. "I didn't. That's what I was trying to tell you last week before you got all crazy about wizards and sidetracked my whole story."

Dana started to say something, but didn't.

"I was out there on the curb, and I couldn't do it. I love these books. I hate their author—he's a criminal and a psychopath—but his books are really good. And I had a hunch that I would need them again."

Dana nodded solemnly.

"And as usual my hunch was right."

Dana rolled his eyes, but Steve was already flipping through the handbook. The book had survived a lot of heavy-duty sleuthing. It was waterlogged and swollen to twice its original size, and its spine was creased and flimsy, but it felt good in Steve's hands. When Steve found his page, he shoved the book in front of his chum's face:

All aboard! When Shawn and Kevin need to sneak around a train, they don't just walk through the cars. Even if the halls aren't full of bruisers and finks (which they probably are), there are too many porters trying to serve them lemonade. That's distracting!

Instead they make like any good sleuth and climb on the roof! It's the fastest way to get from A to B, plus there's plenty of elbow room if you need to throw a haymaker! Sure, it may seem scary, standing atop a locomotive hurtling at 100 m.p.h. But science says everything's swell: The Baileys banish vertigo by recalling the equations they learned in Mr. Rooney's physics class:

$$INITIAL\ MASS \times INITIAL\ VELOCITY$$
$$=$$
$$FINAL\ MASS \times FINAL\ VELOCITY$$
$$[cons.\ of\ momentum]$$

and

$$(1/2)\ INITIAL\ MASS \times INITIAL\ VELOCITY^2$$
$$=$$
$$(1/2)\ FINAL\ MASS \times FINAL\ VELOCITY^2$$
$$[cons.\ of\ kinetic\ energy]$$

See? Train walking is a cakewalk!

Dana obviously didn't like what he was reading. Steve preempted his chum's doubts. "Okay, so here's the plan," he said softly. "We go out a window, one at a time. I'll give you a boost up there, and—"

"Why am I going first?"

"Because you're taller, and you have better balance."

"Right."

"I *said* I'm giving you a boost. This is fifty-fifty here."

Dana slumped. "Seems dangerous."

"Didn't you see the equation? So I give you a boost up there, and then you can help me up. Then we'll run back to the phantom car and figure out how to get in."

"Wait, how are we getting in?"

Steve didn't have time for this. "I just said, we'll figure it out."

"This isn't really a plan."

"We're *planning* to figure it out when we get up there."

"Okay," said Dana. "Then how are you *planning* to open the window? The train is air-conditioned." Dana rapped on the window twice to emphasize his point.

Steve bit his lip. His chum was right. The window didn't open.

"Okay. New plan. We have to distract the conductor. You're going to pull the emergency brake—"

"Of course," Dana said.

"And then fake an injury."

"What kind of injury?"

"I don't know. A broken leg or a heart attack or something. You figure it out. What's important is that you're going to have to keep the conductor distracted. If he tries to leave to find a doctor or something, engage him in conversation—"

"While I'm having a heart attack."

"Meanwhile I'll go back there and get in the phantom car."

"But I thought the conductor said there was no way inside it."

"But obviously he was lying. Because Claire is inside it, right? Once I get in there, I might have to kayo some guys, so don't think you're the only one who has it hard. I mean, all you have to do is fake an injury. Actually, if you can figure out how to slip away after you get the conductor up here, then you could come back and help me fight all these baddies. . . ."

"I don't know about this," Dana said.

Steve was putting the handbook back in his suitcase. "Got any better ideas?"

Dana pointed up to a white button next to the

air-conditioning nozzle. "Why don't we just push that and call the conductor?"

Steve stared at the button and tried to think of a reason Dana's plan wouldn't work.

"Because when he gets up here and sees that our seats are empty and our button's lit up, he'll get suspicious."

"So push Rick's."

Steve paused with the lid of his suitcase halfway closed. "That might work."

Dana smirked.

"Look," Steve said, "that's basically the same idea I just had. Here we go, chum."

"Don't call me chum," said Dana.

Steve shut his suitcase, slipped into the aisle, and hit Rick's button.

CHAPTER XXIII

THIS WAY FOR DANGER

THE BUTTON'S CLICK woke Rick up. Steve backed across the aisle and bumped into his seat's armrest.

Rick yawned and stretched. "Stevie Brix!" he said. He looked expectantly at the boys. "Get it?"

"Get what?" Steve asked.

"Stevie Brix." Rick looked at Steve and then Dana like he couldn't believe what was happening. "Stevie Brix?"

"Like Stevie and then the first part of my last name?"

"No! I guess you're too young for the reference. Too bad. That was a pretty good joke."

Steve doubted it. But he needed Rick's coopera-
tion, so he laughed anyway.

"There you go," said Rick. "So what's going on,
my man? Where you going with that suitcase? You
know this train's moving, right?"

"Dana and I are just going to go find this girl I met
earlier in the café car."

"Oooooooohh," Rick said.

"It's not even like that," said Steve.

"Sure. Sure." Rick held his hand up. "Okay. That's
cool. Very cool."

Steve and Dana started walking.

"Just don't leave the train!" Rick called after them,
and laughed.

Steve laughed too, and then Dana did.

When they got to the back of their car, Steve ducked
into the last row of seats.

"Wait here," he said, pulling Dana down after him.

Steve looked out the window.

"What are we doing?" Dana asked, but Steve
waved the question off.

Thirty seconds later the conductor entered their
car. He passed by the boys and walked up to Rick.
Rick looked confused.

"Now," Steve said. He and Dana jumped into the
aisle and exited the car. They hurried back, back, back

through the cars until they stood in front of the orange sticker that said DANGER.

Dana eyed the sign.

Steve tried to lighten the mood. "Let's hope there are no boggarts back there."

"Balrogs," said Dana.

"Whatever," said Steve. "Come on. Let's go."

CHAPTER XXIV

THE SECRET PANEL

TINY VESTIBULES connected all the cars on the Sunset Coastliner. These little compartments were the joints that held the train together. Passengers traveling between cars had to pass through a noisy no-man's-land: on one end the door they'd just come through, and on the other the door they would enter. Steve liked these little spaces, all gleaming metal curves; they were the only parts of the train that didn't feel cheap.

Steve and Dana stood in the vestibule and stared at the phantom car. From out here it looked just like every other car on the train—shiny and lined with rivets—except for one thing: There wasn't any door.

"There's no door!" Dana yelled above the roar of the tracks.

"I *see* that!" Steve said.

"Looks like the conductor wasn't lying!"

Steve wasn't ready to admit that. He felt the smooth wall, pushing and pressing and tapping.

"What are you doing?" Dana asked.

"Looking for a secret panel!"

The train swung around a corner. Steve stumbled.

"Come on!" said Dana. "There's no secret panel!"

The train rocked, and Steve fell face-first into the wall of the phantom car. His cheek pressed against the smooth metal. Steve secretly hoped his fall would trigger a secret panel. It didn't.

"There must be some way into this car!" Steve said.

Steve was getting frustrated.

He banged his head against the wall.

This also did not trigger a secret panel.

Behind Steve, Dana shouted something.

"What?" Steve asked.

Before he could turn around, a large hand grabbed Steve by the back of his neck.

Someone had entered the vestibule from the Death Valley car.

The grip on Steve's neck was tight, and it hurt.

Steve threw his elbows behind him. They hit some-body, but the grip did not loosen.

Steve tilted his head back and looked up at the chin of the scar-faced man, who had Dana in an iden-tical hold with his left hand. Dana gave Steve a look that said, *This is all your fault.*

His hands still gripping the boys' napes, the man shuffled forward a bit and kicked a rivet with a scuffed brown shoe. There was a pneumatic hiss, and a piece of the wall slid open.

Steve gave Dana a look that said, *I told you there was a secret panel.* The man tightened his hold when Steve turned his head. Steve winced.

Saying nothing, the scar-faced man pushed the boys forward, through the doorway, and into the phantom car.

The secret panel slid closed behind them.

CHAPTER XXV

CAPTURED!

IT WAS QUIET, AND DARK, and Steve opened his eyes wide while they adjusted.

"Let us out of here!" Steve said.

"Shut up," the man said. "Walk."

They were in a narrow corridor lit by a dim yellow lamp encased in a wire cage on the ceiling. The walls were metal, painted light green, and full of handles and hinges.

The man released Dana and Steve and shoved them forward. The hallway required them to proceed single file. Steve considered bolting, shoving his way past the man, and escaping the car. If he and Dana worked together—

"Don't even think about it." The man's voice came out as a nasty slurry of anger and menace.

Steve stopped thinking about it. He walked.

Stenciled letters on the wall said things like SWITCH BOX and ICE-ACTUATED COOLING SYSTEM and CONDUCTOR'S VALVE FOR EMERGENCY ONLY. Two wood doors were closed on Steve's right. Classical music played faintly somewhere ahead.

And then the corridor ended. Steve stood in front of a wide door.

"Go ahead," the man said. "Go."

Steve turned the brass knob and pushed.

The door opened into a spacious, well-lit, wood-paneled room. It was probably the acest place Steve had ever seen. Huge windows revealed a sandy beach to the right and a sloping green hill to the left, both passing by at tremendous speeds. Plush sofas, overstuffed chairs, and tables with elaborate reading lamps lined the walls. It looked like an illustration right out of a Bailey Brothers book.

There were three people in the compartment. Steve took in the scene in the seconds before they all looked up at him. A woman sat playing the cello. A thin man with a mustache relaxed in an overstuffed club chair. And on the sofa, reading an old brochure, was Claire Marriner.

It looked just like an illustration in a book.

CHAPTER XXVI

A STRANGE CAR

"CLAIRE!" Steve said.

The woman stopped playing. The man stood. Claire looked up from the brochure.

"Steve!" she said brightly. Steve was happy that she was happy to see him.

"You know these guys?" asked the scar-faced man.

"Just Steve," said Claire.

"This is Dana," said Steve.

"Hi, Claire," said Dana.

"Cyrus, what is going on?" asked the woman with the cello.

"Cy Marriner?" Steve asked, turning around. "You're a private detective?"

The scar-faced man looked confused. "You've heard of me?"

"Nope," said Steve.

"All right, all right," said the thin, mustached man in the club chair. Steve guessed he was about six feet tall and in his fifties. He had a square jaw and was the first man Steve had ever seen wear an ascot in real life. It was yellow and polka-dotted and weirdly didn't look as goofy as it could have. He raised his hand. "Let's all quiet down and sort this out. Cyrus, who are these boys?"

"I caught the blond one snooping around the train back in Santa Lucia, Mr. V.," Cy Marriner said. "And just now, when I was coming back, I found him and his little friend trying to force their way into this car."

"And?" asked the thin man.

"What do you mean, 'and?'" said Cy Marriner. "Seems pretty suspicious."

The thin man chuckled. "Cyrus. They're just children. They could hardly be car thieves—they don't even know how to drive."

"Actually, I do," said Steve.

The man looked surprised. "Well, anyway, I'm sure they wouldn't *steal* a car."

Actually, Steve had, technically. Twice. Once with

Dana and once without. But it seemed better to leave that out right now.

"Now," said the man, "would one of you lads care to tell us why you were loitering outside this car?"

Steve put his suitcase down on the ground and opened it. "I was looking for Claire, to give her this." He pulled *Pride and Prejudice* out and showed it to the man.

"My book!" said Claire, hopping up from the sofa. "Thanks, Steve!"

"A gallant gesture," said the man.

Steve blushed.

The man frowned. "But also the reason I was reluctant to let you leave the car, Miss Marriner. Too much back and forth is bound to attract attention to our little sanctuary." He cheered again. "Ah, well. I suppose fate has delivered you boys here."

"Where is here?" Dana asked. It was a very good question.

CHAPTER XXVII

SURROUNDED BY MYSTERIES

"WELL, YOU SEE, that's a bit of a secret. 'Here' is the observation room of the personal car of J. Nicholas Vanderdraak and Alice Vanderdraak. Who is me. And my wife. It is us. This is our private car. We own it."

"What do you mean, you own it?" Steve said.

Alice Vanderdraak, the woman with the cello, smiled. She had a very pretty smile. Beautiful, even, although Steve never really felt comfortable using the word "beautiful." "It's our own private car. She's called the Medea."

"Built from parts salvaged from the finest cars of the railroad's golden age: Pullmans, Budds—"

He said these names like everyone had heard of them. Steve hadn't.

"—and disguised to look like a modern car from the outside."

"Wow," said Dana, looking around. "This is pretty first-class."

"I call it 'best class.' And it's the only way to travel."

"Yeah," said Steve. "Business class was pretty underwhelming."

"The decline of train travel," said J. Nicholas Vanderdraak, "is one of the great tragedies of the last century."

"Totally! That's what I've been thinking," said Steve. He thought Claire laughed a little, but he didn't see what was funny.

A man at least twenty years older than J. Nicholas Vanderdraak entered the compartment through an entranceway at the rear. He was dressed in a wool suit and a blue cap, and he carried some sort of tiny xylophone in his right hand. After clearing his throat, he removed a little mallet from his right pocket and played four clear notes. "We'll be serving lunch in ten minutes," the old man said.

"Thank you, O'Rourke," said J. Nicholas Vanderdraak. "Boys, would you like to join us?"

"Yeah," said Steve. "Thanks, um, uh . . ."

What should Steve call him? J.? Or Nicholas? Or J. Nicholas?

"Please, Steve, call me Mr. Vanderdraak."

"Thanks, Mr. Vanderdraak."

"Do you need to check in with your parents?" Alice Vanderdraak asked.

"We're not traveling with our parents," Steve said. "We're traveling with Rick. And I told him we'd be gone for a bit."

"Then let's eat!" Mrs. Vanderdraak said. "The dining room is behind us."

There was a warm and ticklish feeling in Steve's stomach. Steve was hungry, and pleasant aromas were wafting through the car—that was part of the tingle. But Steve's stomach knew that there was excitement afoot. A private detective hired by an eccentric, rich couple, talk of car thieves, an ace private train car—something strange was going on, and Steve wanted to know more. He could always feel a good mystery in his gut. But there was something else making Steve feel a little giddy. And even if he wouldn't admit it to anyone, it didn't take a supersleuth to deduce that he was glad to be having lunch with Claire Marriner.

CHAPTER XXVIII

PROFESSIONAL CURIOSITY

"AND THEN THESE BRITISH WARSHIPS would just like block off the fjords, but then these Icelandic fishing-boat captains would charge out of the harbor at full speed. And the captains would get on their radios and be like, 'We'll just ram you if you don't get out of the way,' and the battleships would move at the last minute."

Dana was explaining the Cod Wars to everyone at the table, when Iceland and Britain fought over who had the right to harvest disgusting fish from the Arctic Ocean or something. They were seated in high-backed chairs, Mr. and Mrs. Vanderdraak on one side of the table, Steve, Dana, and Claire on the other. Steve had claimed the seat by the window without thinking, and was both peeved and relieved when Dana, and not Claire, sat next to him. It was a complicated mix of emotions, and Steve decided the best way to deal with it was to ignore Claire for the rest of lunch.

The dining compartment was very peach. The walls were peach and the chairs were peach and there was an arrangement of odorless peach flowers on the center of the table. Steve wondered whether the flowers were real. He tugged at a petal. They were real. The petal came off in his hand. Steve looked up to see whether anyone was watching him. Mrs. Vanderdraak was, but she smiled and winked at Steve as he pulled his hand back and dropped the petal under the table.

"So these cod captains are like big-time war heroes in Iceland," Dana was saying. Mr. Vanderdraak and Claire were engrossed in his story. Steve was bored. He rested his elbows on the white tablecloth and stared at the blur of shrubs and trees rushing by. He'd heard about the Cod Wars at least five times already, plus all this talk of fish was ruining Steve's appetite.

"Well, all this talk of fish is making me hungry," said Mr. Vanderdraak. "Let's order."

He raised his hand, and the old man O'Rourke shuffled over with menus.

"Oh, and we have a children's menu, don't we, O'Rourke?"

"Yes, Mr. V.," said the old man. He produced a small menu shaped like a rabbit. The bunny on the cover was dressed in a tie and suspenders and smiled shyly. It held a crudely painted sign that said CHILDREN'S MENU. Steve was horrified. The menu reminded him of terrible books about romping animals and endless Easter brunches with his grandma.

"J., honey, I think everybody is old enough to order from the regular menu."

"Yes, the regular menu's fine, Mr. Vanderdraak," Claire said.

Mr. Vanderdraak smiled apologetically. "Of course."

Mrs. Vanderdraak put her hand on her husband's. "J. hasn't spent much time around kids." She smiled and added, "But he's a kid at heart."

Mr. Vanderdraak squeezed her hand. "Oh, Apple," he said.

Steve felt uncomfortable but couldn't really explain why. So he just looked down at his menu:

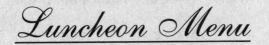

Luncheon Menu

ORANGE *and* GRAPEFRUIT SUPREME

HEARTS *of* CELERY

QUEEN OLIVES

CHEF'S COMBINATION SALAD

Clear Oxtail Soup *with* Sherry
or
Consommé en Tasse, Hot *or* Jellied

Halved Avocado *with*
Sweet Corn *and* Tomatoes
or
Spiced Watermelon Cubes

Marinated Herring *in* Sour Cream

Poached Medallion *of* Salmon,
Sauce Hollandaise

Roast Ribs *of* Prime Beef au Jus

Charcoal Broiled Sirloin Steak

Fried Young Chicken, Maryland

Vanilla Ice Cream *with* Pound Cake

Maple Nut Sundae

Baked Apples *with* Cream

Layer Cake

Cherry Pie

Mr. Vanderdraak held a small pencil and a slip of paper. "We order a bit differently on a train," he explained. "I fill out this card, and it's delivered to the kitchen. Ladies?"

"I'll have the salad and the chicken," Mrs. Vanderdraak said.

"Um," said Claire, "can I have the avocado and the watermelon cubes?"

"Of course," said Mr. Vanderdraak, writing.

Claire looked at Steve. "I'm a vegetarian," she said. Steve nodded. Why had she looked at him?

"I'll have the olives and the roast beef," Dana said.

"And how about you?" Mr. Vanderdraak said. "Your choice, Young Master . . ."

"Brixton," said Steve. He got flustered and ordered the maple nut sundae and the cherry pie.

Mr. Vanderdraak raised his eyebrows and smiled. "You know, I think I'll have the same."

O'Rourke took their order and disappeared through a door at the back of the compartment.

"I think you'll enjoy our meal. O'Rourke is a fantastic cook."

"Where's the kitchen?" Steve asked.

"Behind us. And behind that is our drawing room, and behind that the vault," Mrs. Vanderdraak said.

"The vault?" Steve asked.

Mr. Vanderdraak smiled. "That's just what we call it. We've temporarily converted the guest bedroom into a small cargo space. It's a safe way to transport precious property—nobody robs trains these days."

O'Rourke returned and set the table. The plates and cups and bowls all had the same red pattern:

"Cool dragon," Dana said.

"Yes," said Mr. Vanderdraak. "All the old trains had their own china patterns. The Great Northern had a ram, the Santa Fe California had a poppy—those of us with private cars keep the tradition alive."

"You mean more rich people have cars like these?" Steve asked.

"Oh, sure," said Mrs. Vanderdraak.

"Next time you're on a train trip, take a look at the back car," said Mr. Vanderdraak, chuckling. "You never know when some millionaire's hitched on to your engine."

"I don't really ride trains that often," said Steve.

Dana was still looking at the china pattern. "This is really cool. I'm reading this series right now called—"

Steve interrupted. "Claire, why isn't your uncle having lunch with us?"

"He's working," Claire said.

"Working?" said Steve.

"Yeah, he's—"

"I'm employing Mr. Marriner to look after something of mine," said Mr. Vanderdraak.

"Your car?" said Steve.

Mr. Vanderdraak looked alarmed. "How did you know that?"

"You guys were talking about car thieves earlier."

"Very astute," said Mr. Vanderdraak, looking Steve over. "Wait a second. You said your name was Brixton? Steve Brixton?"

"Yes," said Steve.

"I've heard of you! You're the private detective!"

Steve looked triumphantly at Claire. She rolled her eyes.

"I'm friends with Victor Fairview," Mr. Vanderdraak continued. "Alice, this is the detective who recovered Victor's diamond."

"That's right," Steve said.

"Oh, yes! That was brilliant!" said Mrs. Vanderdraak.

This conversation was getting good. It was hard not to look at Claire again, just to rub it in.

"If we had known you'd be aboard, we wouldn't have needed to hire Mr. Marriner," Mr. Vanderdraak said. "I'm joking, of course," he added. "No offense to your uncle."

"None taken." Claire shrugged.

"Well, anyway," said Steve, "I'm semiretired."

"What does that even mean?" Claire asked.

"Seriously," Dana muttered.

"But just out of professional curiosity," Steve said, emphasizing the word "professional" and ignoring Dana and Claire as they rolled their eyes at the same time, "why have you hired a private detective?"

"Well," said Mr. Vanderdraak, "something very strange has been going on."

CHAPTER XXIX

ONE OF TWO OF A KIND

"You see," Mr. Vanderdraak continued, "I have been having a problem with my cars. Automobiles, I mean—not this train car. Do you know anything about cars?"

"Yeah, sure," said Steve.

Dana looked at him sharply. Steve did not know anything about cars, and Dana knew it.

"Well, I'm crazy about them," Vanderdraak said. "Have been since I was your age: Automobiles were my first love. Not the junk they make these days," he added quickly. "Classics. I have one of the finest private collections in the country, actually. But my problem is that my cars keep getting stolen."

"Our cars, J.," said Mrs. Vanderdraak.

"Yes, Apple," he said, cupping her hand. "*Our* cars keep getting stolen. Of course," he said, "Alice didn't know anything about cars before we were married."

"But I'm learning," she said.

"Yes. Well. We've had six cars stolen from us in the last five years. To have loved and lost . . . ," Vanderdraak said with a sad chuckle. "I've lost two Shelbys, a 2CV, a Tucker, a Bel Air, and a Tucker '48 sedan."

"The Tucker Torpedo!" Steve rose in his chair. "That's the kind of car the Bailey Brothers drive!"

This sentence represented the entirety of Steve's knowledge about cars.

Mr. Vanderdraak looked pleased. "A Bailey Brothers fan! Now there's a lad after my own heart. Those were my favorites when I was a boy. What's your favorite?"

"Um, probably *The Mysterious Lasso*."

"Ah, Bailey Brothers number nine. A masterpiece. But I like number eleven, *The Hidden Hideout*, best."

This guy knew his stuff.

"Were you aware," Mr. Vanderdraak said, leaning over the table, "that the author, MacArthur Bart, doesn't even exist? It's just a pseudonym! The books were all written by ghostwriters."

Steve felt a pang in his chest. "Yeah, I heard that."

Mr. Vanderdraak chuckled. "I think it took me years to recover from that little bit of unwelcome news."

In the back of Steve's mind he felt the itch of unfinished business.

Just then O'Rourke arrived with a heavy silver platter filled with food. He took away the empty plate in front of Steve and three of his four forks, replacing them with a piece of pie and a silver dish full of ice cream. Steve didn't know which to try first, so he put some ice cream on the pie and ate it. It was delicious.

Mr. Vanderdraak talked while the others ate.

"But anyway, we are currently returning from Monterey," said Mr. Vanderdraak, "where I have just acquired the most valuable car in my collection, a 1932 Packard Twin Six Sport Phoebus. I've owned a lot of fine cars, but this one, well, she's special."

Steve had never heard of this car, but it felt like a good moment to whistle appreciatively. Since Steve couldn't whistle, it came out more as an amazed sigh.

"Only two were built, and now I own one of them."

"Where's the other one?" Dana asked.

Yes, that was the question! That must be the reason Vanderdraak had hired Claire's uncle. They were embarking on a search for the other Packard

Whatever Whatever Phoebus—the missing twin, separated at birth—a search that would take them across the world!

"The other car is owned by a collector in Rhode Island," Vanderdraak said.

Steve slumped.

"But the important thing is that one of them is right here. In this train car. That's what we've got in the vault. We're taking it back home. The last robbery occurred when the car was being transported via truck to our estate. The train, I figure, will be safer. But given the fact that I have lately been targeted by a particularly efficient gang of car thieves," Vanderdraak said, "and since the police have been absolutely no help"—Steve nodded sympathetically—"the insurance company insisted that I hire a detective to protect the vehicle. Mr. Marriner apparently specializes in auto theft and comes highly recommended as a consummate professional—which is why I was surprised when he asked to bring along his niece."

"My school's on spring break and he couldn't find a babysitter," Claire said, looking at Steve. She sounded defensive and annoyed, and Steve wanted to tell her she didn't have to explain herself to him, but he looked down at his plate instead.

"Well," Vanderdraak continued, "it's been quite an

exciting journey so far. The police stopped the train at Santa Lucia—apparently an informant had tipped them off to a pair of notorious car thieves operating in the vicinity. They searched the train. But they found nothing."

"I was wondering what was going on," Steve said. "We were waiting at that station."

"Didn't see this man, did you?" Vanderdraak pulled out a sheet of paper from his breast pocket. "They have a mug shot of one of the thieves—the other man is unknown."

Steve studied the paper:

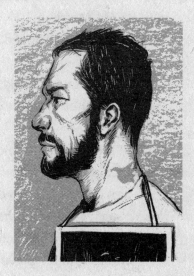

"No," Steve said, studying the picture closely. Dana leaned over and stared at it too.

"Look at that birthmark," Steve told his chum. "It's shaped like a triceratops."

"You mean that?" Dana said. "That looks like an eagle."

"No," said Steve. "There are his two horns, and that's his third horn."

"That looks like wings and a beak."

"Anyway," said Vanderdraak, taking the paper and returning it to his pocket. "I'm comforted that you haven't seen him. You know, it's a shame you're semi-retired, Steve. You could have been a backup pair of eyes for Mr. Marriner."

"My uncle doesn't need another set of eyes," Claire said.

"I'll take the case," said Steve.

Everybody at the table looked stunned. Especially Dana.

"You retired," Dana said.

"Ridiculous," Claire muttered.

"I don't think we need two detectives, do you, dear?" said Mrs. Vanderdraak.

"I don't know, Apple, could be—"

"I'll do it for free," Steve said. "In exchange for pas-sage on the Medea."

"Accepted," Vanderdraak said, grinning widely.

"Great," said Steve.

"Tell you what, as soon as you boys clean your plates, how'd you like to see one of the most expensive automobiles in the world?"

CHAPTER XXX

PHOEBUS

"So HERE'S THE KITCHEN," said Mr. Vanderdraak, leading them back to the rear of the car. They walked in a line: Mr. Vanderdraak, Dana, Steve, and Claire. Mrs. Vanderdraak had stayed in the observation room and was playing the cello—the deep strains echoed in the tiny kitchen where they now stood. "A bit small, but I think you'll agree that O'Rourke here makes good use—"

"Does this guy ever stop talking?" Claire whispered to Steve.

Steve looked back. He rolled his eyes and nodded his head, even though he kind of liked Mr. Vanderdraak.

"—and now, if you'll follow me," Mr. Vanderdraak said, exiting the kitchen.

"Plus he's a total chauvinist," Claire whispered.

"Wait, what?" Steve asked.

"He never offered to show me this car. I think he's glad to have some boys around."

"Are you into cars?" Steve asked.

"No, but neither are you."

"How did you know?"

Claire's expression broke into a wide smile. "I just guessed! But I was right!"

Steve turned around and hurried after Dana.

They were in another cramped hall.

"On your right is the lavatory, dressing room, and sauna," Vanderdraak said, gesturing toward a door.

"Sauna!" Steve said. "You guys have everything."

"Yes," said Mr. Vanderdraak, trying to conceal his smile by nervously brushing his mustache.

"And now the vault." Mr. Vanderdraak stopped before a steel door. He spun a large dial right, left, right and then pulled a large latch. Mr. Vanderdraak threw his weight against the handle and slid the door open.

"Beautiful, isn't she?" Mr. Vanderdraak said. "The Phoebus."

The whole car gleamed. Steve had seen cars like

this in old movies—it looked like it should have tommy guns poking out its windows, or a fur-clad heiress behind the wheel. Instead the car looked too big for the small room, like a burly detective bound and stuffed in some hideout's tiny cellar. The Phoebus was low and long, and all of it sparkled. The body was black and chrome, and the tires were white; if it weren't for the tiny red circles at each wheel's hub, it could have been a black-and-white picture of an old car. The front and back seats were covered with white cotton sheets—"to protect the interior during the trip," Mr. Vanderdraak explained. He pulled back a corner of one sheet carefully, like he was unwrapping a Christmas present, to show off the tan leather upholstery. Mounted on the hood was a chrome angel, wings blown back, holding out a car tire in her slender outstretched arms. It would have seemed like a stupid thing for an angel to carry if it didn't look so pretty.

Steve was simultaneously compelled to touch the Phoebus and terrified of touching the Phoebus. He took half a step toward it.

A man rolled out from underneath the car. Steve leapt back.

"Hello, everyone," the man said, chuckling.

"This is Chuy," Mr. Vanderdraak said. Chuy waved. "He's the best mechanic there is—at least the best I've ever known."

Chuy was tall, or long, since right now he was on the ground. He had a goatee and friendly eyes, and his face was smeared with grease. "She's looking good, *jefe*."

"Fantastic."

Chuy stood up and wiped his hands on his denim jumpsuit. "I'm going to grab some food from the kitchen," he said.

"Of course," said Mr. Vanderdraak. "Well, what do you boys think?"

"The Phoebus won't be stolen as long as I'm here," Steve said.

"Or my uncle," Claire added.

"Well, I'm not sure how you want to proceed, Steve," said Mr. Vanderdraak.

"Well," said Steve. "I guess I just wait around for someone to steal the car."

"Indeed," said Mr. Vanderdraak. "Well, in the meantime, feel free to enjoy the observation room, help yourself to some more pie—"

"What about the sauna?" Steve asked.

"What about it?" said Mr. Vanderdraak.

"Can we use it?"

Mr. Vanderdraak looked surprised. "Yes. All right. Why not?"

"Dibs!" Steve raised a finger into the air.

Dana and Claire looked at each other.

"Fantastic," Vanderdraak said. "You'll find towels and robes in the dressing room." He moved around to the back of the car and wiped a speck of dust off a taillight.

"He never let me use the sauna either," Claire said.

"That's probably because you never asked," Steve said. Man, she could be frustrating.

CHAPTER XXXI

LUXURY . . . AND DANGER!

STEVE, CLAD IN A SOFT WHITE ROBE with a red dragon stitched on its pocket, admired himself in the mirror. He was standing in front of a row of stainless-steel sinks. In his periphery a blur of blue and green and tan flashed in the window. This was how to travel on a train.

Towels, neatly folded like little sailboats, lined the sinks' backsplash. Amber bottles of lotions, salves, and aftershave stood on the counter. In a basket were paper packets labeled SHOWER CAP. Steve had never worn a shower cap before, but suddenly wearing one seemed very important. He took one out and placed it on his head. Yes. This was luxury.

The door to the sauna stood open. He pressed the ON button on the wall, walked into the steam room, and pulled the door closed.

The sauna was a small room covered in light blue tile. There were no windows; yellow light came from a circular lamp on the ceiling. It was quiet in there. The only sounds were the slapping of Steve's bare feet on the floor and an occasional drip. It smelled a little musty, and a little like chlorine.

There was a high ledge against the wall. Steve took a seat and waited.

A thermometer on the wall read 70 degrees.

Then all at once came the sound of steam rushing through pipes. Vapor came gurgling from a vent in the floor and swirled upward. Steve sighed. He relaxed as hot fog gradually filled the room.

Steve wished Claire could see him now, in his nice robe and shower cap, just relaxing and looking cool while steaming it up in a high-end sauna. He tried out various cool-looking poses—elbows on knees, one arm resting on the ledge beside him, head against the wall like a thoughtful man at peace. This was the life.

Then it started getting really hot.

The thermometer read 85 degrees, but it was hotter than any 85-degree day Steve had ever experienced. Must be the humidity. Steve's knees were sticky and wet.

The air felt thick in his throat and lungs. Steve coughed. Did people actually enjoy this? It wasn't pleasant, exactly. It was kind of like being inside a dog's mouth.

Maybe he was missing something. He would give it a few minutes, see if it got better.

Pipes rumbled. Steam kept swirling up from the floor. Steve couldn't see the thermometer anymore. The robe felt damp and heavy and oppressive. Steve was being oppressed by his robe! He was getting loopy. Steve removed his robe. He felt better for fifteen seconds, and then he was hot again. His whole body was soaked. Was it sweat or condensation? Steve was not a big sweater. He prided himself on that. But now his back was slippery and slid against the tiles. Drips from the ceiling fell onto Steve's lap. He felt exhausted. How could sitting around be such hard work?

He hated to admit it, but it had to be said: Steve Brixton was not a sauna guy. He stood, and when he did, he felt hotter. He needed to get out of here: take a cool shower, maybe relax in his robe a little bit. He stepped over to the door, turned the handle, and pushed.

The door was locked from the outside!

CHAPTER XXXII

TRAPPED!

STEVE PUSHED AGAIN.

The door wouldn't budge.

He stepped back, still holding the handle, and threw himself against the door.

It didn't budge.

His mind, dulled by the heat, began to race.

He went to the thermometer and wiped water droplets off the glass. It was now 102 degrees. The heat was unbearable. He shook his head.

What could he do? He needed to get out. He felt along the wall for some sort of opening. The tiles were warm, and they were all Steve could feel. Right. That

Steve felt like a potted lobster.

was the point. The room was sealed except for the vent in the floor: Steam came in, and nothing came out.

Maybe he could turn the sauna off from inside.

He couldn't.

Why would they put the controls on the outside of the steam room?

The thermometer climbed to 103.

Steve was trapped. He felt faint. And he wasn't sure how much longer he could last.

CHAPTER XXXIII

DEADLY HEAT

THE BAILEY BROTHERS' DETECTIVE HANDBOOK has no advice on what to do if you're trapped in a sauna, but it does have a bit to say about locked rooms:

Rats! Even careful crime solvers like Shawn and Kevin Bailey sometimes get caught by baddies. But locks can't keep these two sleuths off the case for long! After they've escaped from their binds using the Old Flex-Your-Muscles-While-You're-Getting-Tied-Up Trick (p. 56), they drape the ropes around themselves

like they're still all tied up! Then they
wait for their no-good captors to come in
with a meal or snack. As soon as those
crooks unlock the door, they bum-rush
the bums and kayo their way to freedom!

Steve doubted the person who had locked him in
this sauna would be coming by with a snack. Someone
wanted him dead. Maybe the baddie would come to
make sure the job was done, but Steve couldn't wait
that long.

He banged on the door. It was solid cedar, and the
knocks were muffled. He shouted until he was too light-
headed to continue. It was useless. Everyone was in
the observation room, listening to Mrs. Vanderdraak
play the cello. How could they hear him, through the
dressing room, through the kitchen and dining compartment, over the noise of the train and the music?

Steve's skin was starting to sting. His head
throbbed. It expanded until it felt like it would fill the
room, and then contracted quickly. His scalp tingled,
and his ears burned. The heat was worst at his head,
and he needed his head to think.

Even more steam hissed from the floor and filled
the sauna. Steve hated that vent. He watched the
steam rise.

Wait. That was something: Heat rises. That was like fourth-grade science. It was why his room on the second floor was so unbearable in the summer. (It really didn't seem fair that Steve had the hottest room in the house, but his mom always said that his heat problem didn't seem like an emergency. Which, okay—given current circumstances, she was totally right.)

Steve dropped to the floor, curling his body and positioning himself as far from the hissing vent as he could. It was cooler down here. Much cooler. But not cool. Still uncomfortably hot, actually—but livable. The vent let out another blast of vapor. Steve's back smarted. He pulled the robe off the ledge and covered himself with it. That was better. How long would it be until someone came to check on him? Ten minutes? Twenty? He could make it that long down here. But what if it was the assassin who opened the door, the one who had trapped him in here? Steve lay on the tile floor of the sauna and hoped that when the door opened, he would still have the strength to mount a credible bum-rush, or at least to run out screaming for help.

CHAPTER XXXIV

OUT OF THE FRYING PAN . . .

STEVE DIDN'T HAVE TO WAIT LONG. Maybe three minutes passed before he heard the door to the sauna open. A rush of cool air filled the room.

Steve tensed; he arched his back, ready to pounce. He wondered if there was some way he could get the robe on himself and pounce in the same move. Otherwise this could be a very embarrassing fistfight.

But he didn't need to. Mrs. Vanderdraak called out, "Steve? Steve! Are you all right?"

Steve lifted a flap of terrycloth near his eyes and peeked out at a pair of red shoes. "I'm okay," he said.

Mrs. Vanderdraak bent down. "Steve, what's going on?"

"Someone just tried to murder me is what's going on."

Alice Vanderdraak's eyes grew big. "Murder you? What do you mean?"

"I mean someone tried to take me out by locking me in the steam room."

"But Steve," said Mrs. Vanderdraak, "the sauna door doesn't lock." Steve looked at the door. It was true. There was no lock.

Mrs. Vanderdraak stood, hurried over to the sink, and filled a glass with cold water.

"Here, you need to drink something," she said, handing it down to Steve, who'd wrapped himself in the robe while she'd had her back turned. He sat on the floor and gulped it down.

"We need to get you to the hospital," said Mrs. Vanderdraak, placing a cool hand against Steve's forehead, like his mom did when he had a fever.

"I'm fine," Steve said. He was barely paying attention. His mind was busy unraveling what had just happened.

"Are you burned?" asked Mrs. Vanderdraak.

"No," Steve said.

"You were gone for a while. I came in to check on

you, and the temperature was set to one hundred and seven degrees. You're lucky you weren't scalded."

Steve stood. "Someone must have been holding the door shut."

"What? Who would—Steve, the room was empty when I came in here. Steve, sit down. The heat—"

"And nothing was blocking the door?"

"No. It did stick a bit." She looked annoyed. "It's old. Like everything on this thing. Look, Steve, sit down. We should really take you back to your—Rick." Just then Claire and Dana peeked their heads in through the dressing-room door. Did Claire know that Dana had a girlfriend? It seemed important that she know that. Steve cinched his robe and stood up.

"Careful, Steve," Mrs. Vanderdraak said. But he felt stable.

"What's wrong?" Dana asked.

"Someone just tried to assassinate me," Steve said.

Dana and Claire looked surprised.

"He got stuck in the sauna," Mrs. Vanderdraak said.

"That's one theory," Steve said, striding around the dressing room. He ran cold water in a sink and splashed it on his face.

"Why would someone want to assassinate you?" Claire asked.

"To get me out of the way."

He turned off the tap.

"Dana," Steve said, talking fast now. "Did you just come from the observation room?"

"Yeah," he said.

"And you were in there with Claire and the Vanderdraaks?"

"Yeah."

"And you didn't see anyone come through there, did you? No goons or anything?"

"No," Dana said, looking grave.

"Then that means the assassin who did this has got to be in the rear of the car."

"With the Phoebus," Dana said.

"Stealing it," Steve said. "Right now."

"Wait. Steve!" said Mrs. Vanderdraak. But Steve was running from the vault, and Dana and Claire were right behind him.

CHAPTER XXXV

A SINISTER FIGURE

ANY REMNANTS OF STEVE'S HEADACHE had vanished by the time he reached the vault door. It was ajar, but only slightly. The three kids were crowded into the corridor.

"We might have to kayo some guys in here," Steve said, remembering the goon in the mug shot from the police. That guy looked pretty tough.

"We're not really good at that," Dana said.

Steve said nothing.

"What do you mean, 'kayo'?" Claire asked.

"Kayo. Knock out," Steve said.

"Oh," said Claire. "That's sort of dumb."

He was beginning to wish she weren't along. He pushed against the vault door. It opened slowly. Dana helped. It opened faster. Steve stopped and let Dana do the work. He stood in the entryway clenching his fists.

The Phoebus was still in the vault. That was the good news. But the bad news was that a goon was in there too.

The goon was standing on the other side of the Phoebus, by the driver-side door. Steve could tell he was a goon right away because he was wearing a stocking over his face. That was pretty much standard-issue goon wear. He looked up as the door opened. Steve couldn't see the crook's face— that was the whole point of the stocking—but Steve imagined his expression was a mixture of surprise and menace.

"Stop it right there!" Steve said, but at that point the thief had already frozen. Without thinking, Steve charged the man. Well, sort of charged. More like carefully skirted around the car toward the man.

The masked man backed up and crouched down low.

"Guard the door," Steve said to Dana and Claire. "Don't let him out."

Steve was at the front of the Packard, near the

hood ornament. His heart was beating fast. He had no idea what he was going to do next.

The man looked desperately around the compartment. He fixed on a pile of Chuy's tools in the back corner of the room. In one swift motion he reached back and stood up with a small lead pipe in his left hand.

"Look out!" said Claire. "He's got a lead pipe!"

"I know!" Steve said.

The villain threatened Steve with the pipe.

Steve stopped where he was.

Then he took a couple steps back toward Claire and Dana.

The thief watched Steve retreat, his gloved fist still wrapped around the pipe.

"What do we do now?" Dana asked.

"Well, he's trapped, right?" said Steve.

"I'll go get my uncle," Claire said.

"No!" said Steve. "Stay here. It's three on one right now. I'm not sure Dana and I could take him if he made a break for it."

The masked man seemed to consider whether or not to force his way through the vault's door. Then he turned toward the back wall and fiddled with a dial Steve hadn't noticed before. Most of the back wall of the compartment swung up and open like a garage door.

A goon!

"Two secret panels!" Steve said, looking at Dana.

Dana frowned at Steve. "That doesn't really count as a secret panel. It must be how they get the car in and out."

The goon looked back at the kids one last time. Behind him train tracks rapidly receded. The man's tank top rippled in the wind. He turned again, took two steps, and jumped.

CHAPTER XXXVI

THE MAN IN THE MASK

"HE'S GONE!" Claire said.

"Where'd he go?" Dana asked.

Steve ran to the back of the compartment and looked out.

"There's a little ladder out here!" Steve shouted above the noise of the train and the rushing wind. "He climbed on top of the train!" After considering, he couldn't help adding: "Told you people did that, Dana!"

Dana and Claire hurried over. The three of them looked at the ladder. It started halfway up the back of the car and continued to the top.

"What do we do now?" Claire said.

Steve looked at her seriously. "We go after him."

Dana slapped his own forehead.

Steve counted to three, then upped it to five, and grabbed a metal rung with his hand. He tried to pull himself up, but his arm was shaking a little, and he'd never been that good at chin-ups anyway. "Dana! I need a boost," he said.

Dana, shaking his head, made a cradle with his hands. Steve couldn't back out now, not with the goon on the loose and everyone watching. He stepped into Dana's hands with a bare foot, counted to six this time, and swung himself over to the ladder. He was on!

Steve tried not to think about the ground moving fast below him. The wind blew his shower cap, which made a plasticky flapping sound. His robe whipped around him. His bare feet curled around a metal rung. This was no time to wish for a more sensible outfit or even a pair of shoes. A chase was afoot.

Still, Steve had to admit this was probably the stupidest thing he'd ever done.

Steve ascended the ladder quickly. It was a surprisingly easy climb. When he peered over the top of the car, he found himself face-to-face with the masked goon. The man was perched like a gargoyle on the roof of the train. When he saw Steve, he reared up and swung the pipe at Steve's head.

Steve ducked.

"What's going on?" Dana shouted from the vault.

Steve didn't answer. He looked up, waiting for the man's second attack. It didn't come. Steve risked another peek. The goon was running forward, toward the engine. He was already on the next car and moving fast. Steve marveled. It looked easy. The goon leapt over the space between cars and kept moving.

Steve looked back down at Dana and Claire, who looked up at him.

Steve couldn't let this crook get away. He climbed up.

CHAPTER XXXVII

HOT PURSUIT

STEVE SLID BELLY FIRST onto the roof of the car, like a
dolphin coming up to kiss a tourist at a marine park.
It wasn't pretty, but it felt secure. He wriggled forward
until his whole body was atop the train.

Steve lay prone on the roof of the train. Okay. This
wasn't so hard. The masked man had run and jumped
without any problem. And Steve remembered a picture he'd seen of a train in India with a bunch of kids
hanging out on top of it. He got up on his hands and
knees. This was doable.

Steve stood.

This was maybe not doable. Steve wobbled a little. He
did not have his train legs. Things felt suddenly windier

and less stable. Plus the train's metal roof was hot on the soles of his feet. Steve collapsed onto all fours again.

Much better. Steve crawled forward. He pulled the robe's sleeves down to cover his palms. Heat from the roof radiated through the terry cloth and warmed his hands and knees. The wind roared by, and the train clattered furiously along the track below.

A steep hillside rose up on Steve's left. Scraggly trees and shrubs passed by too quickly. On his right, the sea.

Steve reached the space between the end of his car and the start of the next. The gap was much smaller than he'd thought it would be. He was able to put his hands on the forward car and leapfrog over.

Steve kept crawling.

The masked man had stopped moving. He stood there, just watching Steve, two cars ahead. He still had the pipe.

It occurred to Steve that he had no plan.

As he crawled the length of the car, he tried to figure out how he would deal with the man holding the pipe. He decided there was only one sensible option. Once Steve reached him, he would stand up. The man would then swing the pipe at Steve's head. Steve would duck at the right moment. His attacker would whiff, lose his balance, and fall off the side of the train.

Yes, that was the new plan.

When Steve looked up again, the goon was coming

forward. Fast. He was already only one car away and would reach Steve in just a few seconds.

So the new new plan was to stand up now. The man leapt onto Steve's car. Steve stood. The metal seared his soles. His shower cap flew off in the wind. Steve waited as the man approached, slowly now.

The man was just a few yards ahead. Steve watched the pipe.

Steve heard faint shouts behind him.

Dana's voice.

What was wrong? Should he look back?

"Steve!"

Dana sounded frantic.

He had to look back, just for a second. He inhaled and spun his head around fast. Dana and Claire were on top of the train. Dana was crouched low and moving toward Steve; Claire stood on the very back car. Claire was frantically pointing forward. Dana stopped and pointed too.

Were they warning him about the goon? Did they think he was blind?

Steve whirled forward. Before his eyes could refocus on the man and his pipe, he saw what Dana and Claire were pointing at: The front of the train had just entered a tunnel.

CHAPTER XXXVIII

OUT OF TIME

THE BAILEY BROTHERS' DETECTIVE HANDBOOK has some useful tips about tunnels:

> If you're sleuthing on a train, you'll probably end up riding on top of it! And if you're riding atop a train, it will probably go through a tunnel! It's like Murphy's Law, only for trains! As you careen toward the tunnel, don't lose your head: Just hang off the side of the train!

But for Steve there was no time. There wasn't even time for Steve to throw himself flat against the top of the train. The tunnel's masonry loomed behind the masked man, who still faced Steve, unaware of the doom that was now mere yards away. Steve closed his eyes. He clenched his teeth. This would hurt.

CHAPTER XXXIX

PITCH-BLACK

FIVE SECONDS LATER, and Steve was still alive. He opened his eyes, but he couldn't see anything. He was standing on top of the train, in the dark, as it moved through the tunnel.

It occurred to Steve that some tunnels are taller than others.

He let out a thrilled and wild holler, which was lost in the din. So relieved was Steve, so exhilarated by his luck, that he nearly leapt for joy. Then he remembered he was in a tunnel and settled for a low-key arm pump.

In the blackness Steve composed his thoughts.

Going through the tunnel had delayed his clash with the masked man, but soon they would emerge into daylight, and the fight would be back on. The train rocked gently as Steve arranged himself into a crouch. He shuffled rightward a foot and a half. Steve would take advantage of the darkness to prepare a new attack. When the train emerged from the tunnel, he would launch himself at the masked man before he had time to ready his pipe. A pinpoint of light appeared ahead and grew rapidly. The roar of the train hurtling through the tunnel was immense. Steve's leg muscles tensed as he prepared to propel himself into his assailant. The train burst from the tunnel, and everything was bright, blindingly white, and Steve squinted for a moment and looked off to his right. He was losing seconds he didn't have, forfeiting the element of surprise. Steve's eyes hurt, but he forced himself to open them, looked straight ahead, and prepared to throw himself into the man's solar plexus.

The man in the mask was gone.

CHAPTER XL

THE GOON VANISHES

Steve was dumbstruck.

He stared at the place where the man had stood.

Where could he have gone?

Of course! He'd rolled off the side of the train and dangled from the side. Sleuths weren't the only ones who knew that trick. Steve crawled over to the right side of the car and peeked over the edge. Nothing but ground passing by much too fast. Steve jerked his head back. He inched over to the left edge and looked down. Nobody was hanging from that side of the train either.

Steve turned and looked behind him.

The man was not anywhere on top of this train.

Neither were Dana and Claire.

CHAPTER XLI

A DARING RESCUE

Now STEVE IGNORED the train's dizzying speed, the way it rocked on the rails, the heat of its steel roof. There was no room in his brain for anything but panic. Steve ran. He found himself at the end of the train without knowing exactly how he'd gotten there. Peering off the back of the Vanderdraaks' car, he searched for any sign of his friends. Could they survive a fall from the top of the car? The Bailey Brothers jumped off moving trains all the time. But Dana and Claire weren't trained sleuths—Dana had read only half of *The Treasure in Trouble Harbor* before he'd decided it wasn't for him.

He scanned the hillside. He couldn't see his friends. What if they had fallen off in the dark? Already the mouth of the tunnel was just a speck far down the track. He needed to get down, alert the Vanderdraaks, stop the train.

Steve hurried over to the ladder on the side of the train. He turned around and lowered his right leg. It missed the rung. Steve was rushing. He was being sloppy. Steve breathed. His right foot searched for a hold. His toes flexed but found nothing. Steve could feel his pulse in his head. The train swung round a curve, and Steve was thrown to the left. He flattened himself, spreading out his arms to stop his slide. His skin made a terrible noise against the metal.

Now both Steve's feet hung off the back of the car. His forearms burned. His belly heaved. And then Steve felt a hand grab the back of his calf. Steve kicked hard. The hand let go. He pulled himself forward a few inches, and scrambled around to see who had grabbed him.

It was Chuy. He was grabbing the ladder with one hand, his eyes worried but alert. He held out his free arm.

"You crazy, *guey*?" he shouted. "Grab my hand!"

"You crazy, *guey?*"

CHAPTER XLII

FULL STEAM AHEAD

"So we just flattened ourselves before we went through the tunnel," Claire was saying.

"Yeah, we just totally hit the deck," Dana said.

"And then after we came out, we were still lying there, and then Chuy came up and helped us down."

Steve and Claire and Dana sat together on a couch in the observation room of the Vanderdraaks' car. The three of them were just wrapping up their story for Mr. and Mrs. Vanderdraak, who sat, looking worried, across from the kids. Chuy stood close by, shifting bashfully when he was mentioned. Cy Marriner leaned against the wall in the corner, looking angry.

He watched Steve, even though Claire was talking—
Steve felt like Cy had been looking at him more than
the other two ever since they got back in the car. It
made Steve uneasy. He sipped on his watermelon
juice, which had been brought by O'Rourke.

"And the thief?" Mr. Vanderdraak said. "The man
in the mask?"

"Gone," Steve said. "I don't know. Maybe he
jumped off the train or something."

Mr. Vanderdraak pursed his lips. "Yes," he said
quietly.

"I hope you kids know you're lucky to be alive,"
Mrs. Vanderdraak said. "And if it weren't for Chuy, I
don't know what would have happened. Thank you,
Chuy."

"No problem," he said, looking at the ground.

She turned back to Steve. "What were you thinking, charging up there?"

Steve felt defensive. "I was trying to catch the guy
who was stealing your car."

"Yes, well, we've hired a detective to do that," she
said. "An adult detective."

"Yeah, well, the adult detective wasn't around,"
Steve said, looking at Cy.

Cy's eyes narrowed. Steve refused to look away,
even though he wanted to.

"Then you should have told one of us," Mrs. Vanderdraak said. "An adult."

"Yes, where were you, Cy?" Mr. Vanderdraak asked.

"I was up front, checking out the passengers," he said, not quite making eye contact with his boss.

"I want you back here from now on. We're lucky the Phoebus wasn't stolen."

Cy ran his fingernails across the stubble on his face. "And how," he asked, "was this guy going to steal a car from a moving train?"

Steve was surprised when Mr. Vanderdraak looked at him for help. Steve swallowed the last of the watermelon juice to buy some time to think. "Well, I'm guessing there's some sort of ramp back there, to load and unload cargo, right?"

Vanderdraak nodded.

"Lower the ramp and drive off the back."

"Of a train going sixty miles per hour in the other direction," Cy said, shaking his head.

"You got a better idea, Cy?" Steve crossed his arms. "How would you steal the car?"

"Well, I'm just glad everyone's safe," Mrs. Vanderdraak said. "O'Rourke, bring the kids some more watermelon juice."

The gathering broke up soon after that. Chuy and

Cy went back to the vault. Claire pulled out her book, and the Vanderdraaks excused themselves and went to their drawing room. Steve grabbed Dana's arm and pulled him into the corridor by the kitchen.

"What's up?" Dana said, annoyed at being led around.

"The investigation continues," Steve said.

"What are you talking about?" Dana asked.

"Are you serious?" Steve tilted his head and stared at his chum.

"Yeah, I'm serious. I thought you were retired."

"I was. And then I came out of retirement."

"For one last case. To find Claire. Well, we found her." Dana pointed back to the observation room. "So why don't you go talk to her?"

"Why?" Steve asked.

"Please. Dude, she likes you. She told me she thinks you're funny."

Steve wanted to hear more, but instead he said, "So what?" He pulled his notebook out of his pocket. "Check this out. We know whoever tried to kill me in the sauna and then steal the Phoebus is probably someone in this car," Steve said.

"How do we know that?"

"Because he knew how to open the cargo door in the vault. And he was wearing a mask. Why would he wear a mask unless he was afraid we would recognize him?"

"So we couldn't describe him to the police?" Dana said.

Steve thought about that for a second. Dana was getting better at sleuthing. "Yeah, but that's the less likely reason. Anyway, I need to ask you. Before you and Claire joined me and Mrs. Vanderdraak in the dressing room, you were hanging out with her husband in the observation room, right?"

"Yeah."

Steve wrote something in the notebook.

"Steve," Dana said. "This isn't even your case. It's Claire's uncle's."

Steve looked up and smiled. "But what if the detective is also the criminal?"

CHAPTER XLIII

SOUTHPAW

Steve handed his notebook over to Dana. It was opened to this page:

MYSTERY:
WHO TRIED TO KILL ME
AND THEN STEAL THE PHOEBUS?

NAME	MOTIVE	OPPORTUNITY	MEANS
~~Mrs. V~~	????	No. Was with me in the dressing room.	
~~Mr. V~~	Not really. He already owns the Phoebus.	No. He was in the observation car.	
~~Chuy~~	Likes cars. Would make him rich.	No. He rescued us from inside the train.	

NAME	MOTIVE	OPPORTUNITY	MEANS
~~O'Rourke~~	For the money.	Don't know where he was.	No. He is really old
~~Rick~~	Jerk.	Not really. Was probably napping and doesn't even know about the Phoebus.	
Cy Marriner	Jerk and money.	Yes. WHERE WAS HE?	YES.

"Why is Rick on here?" Dana asked.

"Just in case. Anyway that's not important. Cy is the only one with motive, means, and opportunity."

Dana looked impatient. "Okay, but that still doesn't mean he did it. It just means he could have done it. And how would he get back in the train from on top of it?"

Steve chewed on his pen. "I've been working on that. Maybe he slipped down in between cars."

Dana's face was all irritated disbelief.

"Okay, okay. Maybe he has a confederate up in the engine or something. Or someone opened a window."

"Steve. The windows don't open."

"Maybe one window opens."

Dana shook his head. "We still don't have any evidence."

Steve put his hands on his hips. "We have one piece of evidence."

"What."

"He's a southpaw!"

"What?" Dana asked.

"The guy in the mask. He's a southpaw."

"What's a southpaw?"

"It's what the Bailey Brothers call someone who's left-handed."

"Why don't they just say left-handed?"

"Well, they do, sometimes. But I think it's a boxing term. You know, because Shawn Bailey is the best boxer in Benson Bay, except for maybe Kevin Bailey? Anyway, 'southpaw' just sounds cooler."

"Okay, so the guy was left-handed. So?"

"So check this out." Steve headed down the corridor to the vault. Chuy and Cy were talking by the driver-side door of the Phoebus. Both men looked up when Steve and Dana entered.

Steve reached in his pocket and dug out a grape Jolly Rancher. "Hey, Cy," he said. "Want some candy?"

"What?" Cy said.

Steve threw the Jolly Rancher across the car's hood. Cy looked surprised. He didn't move. The Jolly Rancher bounced off his shirt and landed on the floor.

"Careful, *guey!*" Chuy said. "You could hit the car!"

Cy scowled.

Steve turned back toward Dana. "He was supposed to catch it," he whispered.

When he turned back around, Cy was looking at the cargo door. He took out a notebook much like Steve's, opened it, and wrote down some notes.

He wrote with his left hand!

CHAPTER XLIV

THE HOUND WITH TWO TAILS

BACK IN THE CORRIDOR Steve said, "See?"

"Yeah," Dana said. "That's pretty weird."

Steve was triumphant.

"Still," Dana said, "it could be just a coincidence."

"Come on. Do you know what percentage of the population is left-handed?"

"No. What?"

"Like one percent," Steve said.

"I don't think that's true."

"Okay, but it is true."

"How do you know that?"

"I read it in a magazine."

"What magazine?"

"I don't know. *National Geographic*."

Dana waved dismissively.

"Anyway, it's a big clue."

"It's a clue," Dana said. "I don't know how big it is. I mean, this guy is a private detective."

"So what?" Steve said. His throat caught a little. "Look, I'm not sure I trust private detectives a whole lot."

"But you are one."

"Right, but look at what happened with Bart."

"He was just a writer."

"He understood the sleuth's mind better than anyone! All I'm saying is, just because someone is a private detective doesn't mean they're a great person. Even the best detective can go bad."

"Okay. Okay. Calm down. So what do you want to do?"

Steve leaned in and talked low and fast. "The big question is, where does Cy keep going? He keeps leaving the Vanderdraaks' car. I have a feeling that's the key to this whole case. Like I said, maybe he has an inside man on the train. Or maybe one of those car thieves is disguised as a normal passenger. But we need to figure out what he's up to."

"How do we do that?" Dana asked.

"We tail him."

"Don't you think he'll notice? He's a detective, and the train is pretty small."

Steve pulled out *The Bailey Brothers' Detective Handbook*, which he'd stuck in the waistband of his cargo shorts. He showed Dana the section on "Surveillance."

Shawn and Kevin always say, "When you're tailing a crook, it's neat to be discreet!" To make sure your target doesn't catch on to you, always walk with a newspaper in front of your face. That way if the suspect looks back, he won't suspect a thing! He'll just think you're another person walking around and reading the newspaper! (Watch out for parking meters and steep curbs!)

But believe it or not, even the newspaper trick may not be enough to avoid the canniest crooks. If you're tailing a savvy baddie, grab a chum and employ the technique known as the Hound with Two Tails. Here's how it works: One sleuth follows the goon, while another follows the follower. If the followed discovers the follower, the follower's follower now follows the followed, and the original follower follows the follower's follower, who is now simply the follower! You follow?

"Huh?" Dana said.

"I know. It's a little complicated. But basically, I'm going to tail Cy, and then you tail me. And if he sees me, we switch."

"But he'll recognize either of us."

"Yeah, but the Hound with Two Tails has another advantage. You're like backup for me. If I get in any trouble with Cy, then you can come in and save me."

"Save you how?"

"Kayo him!"

Dana winced.

"You'll have the element of surprise," Steve said.

"I don't know," Dana said, but Steve knew his chum was in.

CHAPTER XLV

WATCHING THE DETECTIVE

THE BOYS DIDN'T HAVE TO WAIT LONG. Soon after they finished their conversation in the hall, when they were pouring themselves glasses of watermelon juice in the kitchen, Cy passed by, muttering to himself.

"Give me a head start and then follow," Steve said. He took a gulp from his glass and exited the kitchen.

"Hey, Steve!" Claire put her book down when Steve entered the observation room. "I wanted to ask you—"

"Where's your uncle?" Steve said.

"Oh. Um, he just left. Do you know if—"

"I've got to go check in with Rick," Steve said. "He's

probably worried about me. I'll talk to you later."

Steve left the compartment. When he got to the front of the car, he pushed the button on the wall. The secret panel opened. He walked into the next car.

Cy Marriner was at the front, about to exit through its forward doors. Steve pretended to fiddle with some luggage up on the rack, keeping it really natural. As soon as Cy was through the doors, Steve took off after him.

Steve followed Cy up through the next three cars, past the barking dog and the scarf-necked man, past the passengers napping and typing. Cy was moving fast—he exited through the front of the car. Steve hurried up, almost running down the aisle. He ran straight into an arm that came down across the aisle like a level at a railroad crossing.

Great. It was Rick.

"Whoa, Seabiscuit," Rick said.

"Hey, Rick," Steve said.

"Don't 'hey Rick' me," said Rick. "Where have you been? Huh? I wake up and you and Dana are gone. Are you trying to get me killed by your mom? Are you? Where have you been?"

"I told you," Steve said. "We were hanging out with this girl a few cars back. We kept checking on you but you were still asleep."

"Wrong," Rick said. "Wrong. I just looked up and down this whole train—I didn't see you anywhere. Now do you want to tell me how you disappeared?"

"Did you check the bathrooms?" Steve asked.

"Oh," said Rick. "No."

"There you go," Steve said.

"Wait, all three of you were in different bathrooms at the same time?"

"I don't really feel comfortable talking to you about this, Rick," Steve said.

"Right. Okay. It's just . . . ," Rick said. "With the police back at the station and . . . you know, you being a 'detective,' well, I thought maybe there was a mystery going on or something. Like a case."

Steve laughed. "No way, Rick. We've just been hanging out."

"Right." Rick brightened. "Hanging out. Wait. Where's Dana?"

"Back there." Steve motioned to the rear of the car. "He's coming up to the café car with me."

"Cool, cool," said Rick. "Just don't disappear again!" he said, wagging his finger jokingly.

"Okay," said Steve, and headed toward the business-class car.

By now Cy had gotten way ahead. Luckily, it was a train. There was only one direction he could go. Steve rushed through business class. Maybe Cy was meeting his confederate in the café car. The door at the front of business class whooshed open.

There, crouched in the vestibule between business class and the café car, was Cy Marriner. He stood and grabbed Steve by the shirt, shoving him against the wall. The doors closed behind Steve.

CHAPTER XLVI

THREATS

"WHY ARE YOU FOLLOWING ME?" Cy asked.

Steve was silent. Dana would be arriving soon. That would put an end to this little interrogation. Until then Steve would just let Cy do the talking and see if he ended up incriminating himself.

"I said, why are you following me? Huh?" Cy gave a little laugh. "You think you're onto something, don't you? You think you know my secret? You don't know anything. You don't know anything about me. Look me in the eye. That little trick back there with the Jolly Rancher? You think that proves anything? You got something to prove? You won't prove nothing, okay? And I won't tolerate another detective snooping around, trying to—why do you keep looking at those doors?"

Steve looked Cy in the eye again. Where was Dana? Steve was getting anxious.

Cy broke into a grin.

"Where's your little buddy?" Cy asked. "He following you? You guys pulling a Hound with Two Tails?"

Oh no.

"He coming through those doors? Is that why you keep looking over? It is, isn't it?"

Cy pinned Steve against the wall of the vestibule with his left hand and pivoted to face the door.

Steve had to figure out a way to warn Dana.

Five seconds later the door opened. Cy yanked a surprised Dana by the arm and pulled him into the vestibule.

"We've been expecting you," Cy said to Dana. Dana looked at Steve. Steve looked at Cy. Cy looked both boys up and down.

"Well, here we are again. You two are a couple of real ace sleuths," he said. "Stay away from me. And the Vanderdraaks. And Claire. I don't want to see you again."

He released the boys and walked back into business class.

CHAPTER XLVII

CLAIRE RETURNS

STEVE AND DANA sat in coach class, in their original seats, deliberating about how to proceed with the case. Or, actually, Steve deliberated, while Dana read Wizards' Worlds. Rick knit.

"We've got to get some more evidence and warn the Vanderdraaks," Steve said quietly, so Rick wouldn't overhear him.

Dana read.

"Come on, Dana. The case is heating up!"

Dana read.

"Let's do this!"

Dana snapped his book shut and whispered fiercely

back at Steve. "Did you have fun with Cy up there? I didn't. Do you enjoy being threatened and jerked around? Because I don't. I don't care whether that guy is a car thief or a detective or what. It's not our problem. I don't care if some rich guy's car gets stolen, and neither should you. You're not even getting paid to be on this case. You're just showing off."

"What do you mean?"

"You know what I mean."

Steve's ears felt hot. "No."

"Claire."

"Wrong!" Steve shouted. This attracted Rick's attention.

"What are you guys talking about over there?"

"Nothing," Steve said.

"Nothing, huh? How's that girl, Steve?" Rick asked.

"What girl?" Steve said.

"Ooooohh," said Rick.

Dana laughed.

Just then Claire Marriner came walking up the aisle, hauling Steve's suitcase.

"Hey, Steve," she said. "Hey, Dana."

"Hey, Claire," said Steve.

"My uncle said you guys weren't coming back to our car again, so I brought you your suitcase."

Rick leaned over his armrest. "Aren't you going to introduce us, Steve?"

"Claire, this is Rick."

"I've heard a lot about you, Claire," Rick said.

Claire beamed. She looked at Steve.

"He hasn't," Steve said.

Dana elbowed Steve in the ribs.

This was ridiculous. Steve needed to talk to Claire alone.

"Hey, Claire," Steve said casually, "want to get something from the café car?"

Steve ignored Rick's enthusiastic wink.

Claire cast a nervous glance backward before saying, "Sure."

"Ta-ta, kids," Rick said, smiling knowingly.

Ta-ta.

Who said 'ta-ta'?

Rick.

CHAPTER XLVIII

FIGHT!

STEVE AND CLAIRE sat across from each other at a table, holding paper cups full of hot chocolate.

"I'm so glad to get out of that car," Claire said.

"Really?" Steve said. "I kind of like it."

Claire made a sour face. "It's oppressive. Super rich people are like a different species. Mr. Vanderdraak is such a snob. The way he talks: 'Children, look at my automobile'"—Claire did a pretty good Mr. Vanderdraak impression—"and what kind of first name is J., anyway? And Mrs. Vanderdraak is always playing that cello so badly—"

"Really? She's bad?"

"Well, she's not very good."

"Do you play the cello?"

"No. Piano."

Steve decided he'd like to hear her play some time, and then decided not to tell her that.

"I guess you're right," Steve said. He hadn't picked up on any of this back there.

"Anyway, it's good to be up here for a while. You know, my uncle told me not to hang out with you anymore. He doesn't know I brought you your suitcase."

"Well, that's—"

"He was so angry at me for going up on top of the train. I guess he blames you for that." Claire paused for a second. "He has a point."

"Also he—"

"But I meant to tell you that I thought it was really brave what you did. I mean, it was so scary up there, right? It was fun, but scary. And you were, like, running around, chasing that guy."

"Yeah."

"What were you going to do when you found him?"

"I don't know," Steve said. "I guess I was lucky the tunnel came. Oh, and, um, thanks for pointing out that tunnel and everything. That was really great."

Claire turned pink. "You're welcome."

"But Claire," Steve said. "I have something I want

to tell you." Steve's tongue felt fat, and it was tripping up his words.

"Yes?" Claire asked.

"I think your uncle is trying to steal Mr. Vanderdraak's car."

Claire's face went from red to white. "What?"

"Yeah, I think he's the car thief. Or one of them."

"That's crazy."

"No, I'm serious."

"What gave you that idea?"

"Well, he's left-handed, first of all. And he'd be like an inside man. He's the only person whose whereabouts are unknown when we were on top of the train. It just makes sense."

Claire pushed her chair back. "No, Steve, it does not make sense. I know my uncle, okay? He raised me. We're basically each other's only family. He's not perfect, but he's not a criminal."

"He raised you?" Steve said. "What happened to your parents?"

"They got into a car accident when I was—look, I don't even want to talk to you about this, okay?"

Steve didn't know what to say. This was not going as planned. He was hoping Claire would be impressed with his sleuthing and help spy on her uncle. "Fine," he said. "I didn't think you'd be so mad."

"Of course you didn't! You just thought about yourself and your case." Claire stood up. "No wonder you and my uncle don't get along. You're so similar. Good-bye, Steve Brixton." She stormed out of the café car. Her hot chocolate was still on the table.

Steve reeled. He felt terrible. And shocked. It was like in Bailey Brothers #43: *The Clue of the Curse of the Inca Blade*, when Shawn and Kevin opened the door to their hotel room and it was full of jaguars. How was Steve supposed to know Claire would react like that? Cissie Merritt and Hannah Fenway never yelled at the Bailey Brothers. Still, Claire was more interesting than either of those two. Although it could be so hard to talk to her. Plus Steve didn't even know whether he'd ever see Claire again. She'd said his first and last name when she said good-bye. That was never a good sign. And anyway, Steve didn't even know whether he wanted to see Claire again. In fact he probably didn't.

He sighed.

"Now what?" he asked the abandoned cup across the table.

CHAPTER XLIX

RENDEZVOUS AT UNION STATION

STEVE SPENT THE REST OF THE TRIP looking out the window while Dana read and Rick knit. It was a relief to not be on the case anymore, to not have to think about what he was going to say to Claire. Or at least that was what he told himself. By the time the train came to a lurching halt in San Diego's Union Station, Steve had gotten good at ignoring the itching at the edges of his brain.

They stepped down off the train and into the late-afternoon heat. The station looked like an old mission, with white walls and red-tiled rooftops. Twin golden spires glinted atop two towers, right next to

a blue and white sign that said, confusingly, SANTA FE.
Steve followed Rick past a row of palm trees, under a
tall arch, and into the station.

The station hall was one long room with mosaic
walls and long wooden benches. The passengers from
the Sunset Coastliner milled about, buying snacks,
hugging family members, or looking lost. People waiting to catch trains watched the new arrivals or lay with
their heads resting on big backpacks.

Rick was over at the information desk, talking
with an annoyed-looking woman while holding a
cell phone up to his ear. He was trying to get walking
directions to the hotel.

Steve and Dana waited under a sign that said
TO TRAINS. Dana had his book out. Steve sat on his
suitcase.

Suddenly Steve stood.

"Dana. Dana! Look at that."

Cy Marriner was standing by a bank of pay phones,
talking to another man. It was the man with the scarf,
only now he wasn't wearing a scarf. His bald head
reflected light from a chandelier overhead.

"So?" Dana said.

"Imagine that guy with a beard and mustache and
a full head of hair."

Dana shuffled a few steps to his left so he could see

past a family posing for a photograph. "Okay. What about him?"

"That's the car thief!"

"Hmm," Dana said. "Maybe."

The two men exchanged a couple sentences and then walked in opposite directions. Cy went over to the station's restaurant. The bald man was coming for Steve and Dana.

Steve yanked *The Masterless Apprentice* from his chum's hands and put it in front of his face. He peered over the book's top as the man walked past them.

"Look," Steve whispered to Dana. "The birthmark."

On the man's neck was a coffee-colored spot.

And then the man was gone, out on the platform.

"Did you see that?" Steve said. "Did you see the triceratops?"

"I saw an eagle," Dana said.

Steve ignored his chum. "This is the proof! Cy's in cahoots with the car thieves!" said Steve. "They're probably going to make an attempt on the Phoebus."

"Should we tell the police?"

Steve shook his head. "Of course not. They won't know what to do—plus if they catch this thief, Cy will deny everything and get away. I've got a better idea—we'll catch the thieves red-handed and figure out where the gang is stashing the rest of the

Vanderdraaks' cars." *And prove to Claire that she was wrong,* Steve thought.

Dana looked dismayed.

Steve looked at Rick. He was walking around in circles, talking on his cell.

"Have you heard of the Wooden Horse?" Steve asked.

"The what?"

"The Wooden Horse."

"Is that like the Trojan horse?"

"No, the *Wooden* Horse. It's a classic sleuthing technique. In *The Clue of the Vanishing Tire Tracks*, Shawn and Kevin are trying to track down a bunch of car thieves. But all the crooks are these really ace drivers, and when the Bailey Brothers chase them, the cars keep disappearing after this blind curve in the road. So Shawn and Kevin use the Wooden Horse: They hide themselves in the trunk of a hot rod and park it where all the cars keep getting stolen. And then the baddies steal the car, and they take it back to their hideout—which is in a sea cave—and Shawn and Kevin bust out, take the gang by surprise, and recover all the cars."

"That is the Trojan horse," Dana said.

"Whatever. The Bailey Brothers call it the Wooden Horse."

"I've never heard it called that anywhere else."

"You're missing the point. The point is we can be heroes and break this case wide open."

Dana took his book back. "I don't know," he said. "It sounds dangerous."

"Of course it is!" Steve said. "Danger is how sleuths know they're on the right track."

Dana thought for a second. "Pass," he said.

"What?"

"Pass. I pass. No thanks."

"But the Wooden Horse!"

"I don't care about the Wooden Horse," Dana said. "I don't care about the Trojan horse. I just want to go to the hotel, meet up with everybody, and give my speech about cod tomorrow."

Steve couldn't believe what he was hearing. "Cod? Cod?" Steve shook his head. "Fine. That's fine. You chose her over me."

"What?" Dana said.

"Other Dana. You'd rather hang out with her than go on this adventure with me."

"That is not what this is about," Dana said.

"I knew this would happen."

"Steve—," Dana said, but Steve wasn't listening. Rick was off the phone and writing something down at the information desk. It was time to act.

"Good luck with the cod," Steve said. "I'm off to ride a horse."

Dana looked puzzled. The line had sounded better in Steve's head.

Steve ran off down the platform, leaving his best friend and his good suitcase behind him.

CHAPTER L

THE WOODEN HORSE

STEVE BRIXTON SAT IN THE TRUNK of a 1932 Packard Twin Six Sport Phoebus. It was dark and cramped, and it smelled like boot polish.

But the plan was going perfectly. Steve had told the station agent that he'd left a book on the train; then he'd boarded on the DEATH VALLEY car, run back, and opened the secret panel. Luckily—and good luck, like danger, was a sleuth's signpost—the Vanderdraaks had been in their drawing room (Steve heard them talking as he walked by). O'Rourke had been in the kitchen, but he was doing the dishes, and his back was to Steve. Chuy was nowhere to be found.

Steve had opened the trunk and climbed on in.

The only thing that could have made this case better was a chum. And another six inches of legroom. Although, given the legroom situation, Steve wasn't sure there was room for a chum in here anyway. How had Shawn and Kevin both fit inside the trunk of a car? The illustration had made it look like there had been so much room.

Now the only thing to do was wait.
Steve waited.

CHAPTER LI

STOLEN

IT WAS HARD TO SAY exactly how long Steve waited. Time passes strangely in absolute darkness. Plus Steve fell asleep for a while. But he woke up to the sound of two men talking outside. The men's words were muffled, but their voices were tense and urgent.

There was the high-pitched whine of metal on metal, and then the car was moving. Steve was thrown against the inner wall of the trunk.

The car was going down the ramp. The Phoebus was being stolen!

The Phoebus's engine rumbled. The trunk rattled. Steve plugged his ears. The car was in motion, driving fast. Steve slammed against the other wall. They were going uphill now. Steve wished he could see what was going on. Then: silence.

The car stopped.

They couldn't have driven very far. The car had been on for no more than ten seconds. And then there was the sound of another engine roaring, not the Phoebus's but one very close by. And now the Phoebus was moving again. The thieves must have driven the car into a truck that was carrying it away. Of course! You couldn't just drive off down the highway in one of the world's rarest cars. People would notice.

Steve's legs were stiff, and the trunk was stuffy, but he was too excited to care much. Steve started counting the seconds so he could estimate how far from San Diego they were traveling. When he got to thirty minutes he figured they'd gone about twenty-five miles. By the time Steve got to forty-five minutes, he was asleep again.

CHAPTER LII

IN THE LAIR

WHEN STEVE WOKE UP, everything was still and quiet. His heart beat fast. The Wooden Horse had worked: The Phoebus was parked in the thieves' den. Steve smiled in the darkness.

Quickly he outlined his next moves. The criminals wouldn't be expecting him, so that was good. Still, there were probably two or three guys, and Cy had a revolver, so Steve didn't like his chances in a fight. He would burst out from the Phoebus and put these crooks under citizen's arrest; if they didn't comply, Steve would use his magnifying glass—nestled in the pocket of his cargo shorts—to scratch or even dent the Phoebus. Then their prize would be worthless. Maybe the baddies wouldn't even be around. They could be out drag racing in a local warehouse district or blowing off steam in some basement gambling operation. In that case Steve would sneak out and notify the police—now that he'd done the cops' work for them—and they could lay an ambush outside the hideout.

Well, there was no point waiting any longer. Steve stretched, flexed his fingers, and took a deep breath.

Go!

Steve realized there was no way to open a trunk from the inside.

CHAPTER LIII

A BOLD PLAN

HE WAS STUCK.

This was a pretty big problem with the whole Wooden Horse concept.

Steve tried to remember how the Bailey Brothers had done it. He was pretty sure they'd just raised the lid and climbed out. Maybe their hot rod was built differently? Steve pressed firmly but quietly against the top of the trunk. He felt around the latch for some sort of release. There wasn't one.

This was not good.

Steve started breathing faster.

Suddenly Steve became conscious of how stale

the air was inside the trunk. Couldn't you run out of oxygen trapped in a car like this? Then again, Steve had lasted this long, so the trunk must not be airtight. Unless the fact that he had been in here a long time was a bad thing, and meant that he wouldn't have much time left.

Every breath felt bad in Steve's lungs. Unsatisfying. Poisonous, even. Was he imagining this? He tried to calm down, to inhale and exhale slowly, but his breaths just became shallow and fast.

Steve's head moved back and forth like he was searching for something around him, but there was no light. His hand groped around on the floor of the trunk. It was empty.

Assuming that there was air, how long could Steve last in here? A couple days without water. Someone would have to come rescue him in the next couple days. And nobody knew where he was.

Dana. Dana knew. Dana would tell Rick, and Rick and the police would have to track down the Phoebus.

Steve didn't like those odds. He would have to think of a new plan.

Steve drummed his fingers on the top of his head, thinking.

He stopped.

There was really nothing else he could do.

Steve started banging on the lid of the trunk. The clanging reverberated around him.

"Hello, criminals!" he shouted. "My name is Steve Brixton, I am a detective, and I am in the trunk of this car. I have infiltrated your hideout and witnessed the commission of a crime. I am placing you under citizen's arrest. Please open the trunk and then put your hands up."

After four minutes of banging he heard someone fiddling with the latch.

Steve balled up his left fist and grabbed his magnifying glass with his right. Would it be Cy, or the bald guy? Steve hoped it was the bald guy—Cy knew a lot of good holds.

The lid lifted, and light poured in.

"Hey, *guey*."

CHAPTER LIV

THE MAN UNMASKED

CHUY STOOD LOOKING DOWN at Steve, who was poking out from the back of the car like a hatchling turtle from an egg. He blinked big slow blinks and looked around him.

He was in a large room or small warehouse, brightly lit by industrial lamps that hung high overhead. The floor was polished cement that reflected the lamplight in spectacular patterns. Arrayed neatly around the Phoebus were six beautiful old cars, including one Steve recognized from countless Bailey Brothers illustrations: a Tucker '48 sedan. In the pictures Shawn and Kevin's souped-up auto, the Jalopy, was usually teetering off a picturesque cliff or swerving to avoid road hazards like rusty nails and bicycle messengers. And although this Tucker Torpedo was freshly waxed and shone like a supermarket apple, the car didn't look right parked in the middle of a windowless room.

"Come on out," Chuy said.

Steve's eyes had started adjusting to the light, and he saw that Chuy was smiling warmly, but also holding a lead pipe in his left hand.

So Chuy was a southpaw.

Steve felt like staying in the trunk. Part of his reluctance to move was due to the sluggish disappointment that detectives always feel when one of their pet theories proves wrong. Mostly it was because of the lead pipe.

But if Steve was going to get out of the mess he now found himself in, the first thing he'd need to do was to get out of the trunk. Steve lowered himself onto the warehouse floor.

"Careful," Chuy said.

Steve stretched. Steve was sore, and the stretching hurt.

"So that was you on top of the train," Steve said, nodding toward the pipe.

"Sure," Chuy said.

"But then how did you get back inside the train to rescue us?"

"When we went through the tunnel," Chuy said. "In the dark I ran back past you and got in the train."

"That's crazy," Steve said.

"Sure, crazy." Chuy was grinning. "My father, he worked for the railroad. My first job was on the railroad too. He taught me"—Chuy used the middle and index fingers of his right hand to mimic running. "I'm good on trains. You? Not so good on trains." Chuy laughed. Steve didn't.

"Well, I guess I should thank you for saving me up there, except you were also trying to hit me on the head with a pipe."

"No. I was trying not to hit you, *guey*. Just scare you."

"Yeah, well, it worked," Steve said. He rubbed his arms to get his circulation working. "So you're the one who's been stealing Mr. Vanderdraak's cars," Steve said.

"Sure," Chuy said.

"Well, that solves this case, then." Steve tried to make his voice sound deeper—if this next bit was going to work, he'd need to sound confident. "Like I said before, Chuy, I'm placing you under citizen's arrest."

Chuy looked confused.

"So drop your lead pipe."

Chuy didn't.

"Because you're under arrest right now."

Chuy smiled. "I don't get it. How can you arrest me? You're not a policeman. You're a kid."

"Yeah, I'm also a detective, but that doesn't matter. It's a citizen's arrest. As a citizen who witnessed a crime, I can arrest you. So right now, legally, you are under arrest and you have to do what I say."

Chuy looked like Steve was telling him a joke. "Sorry, *guey*, but you can't do a citizen's arrest."

"Wrong, Chuy," Steve said. "You're wrong. I have the full backing of the laws of the state of California and the United States of America."

"Sure, *guey*, but you're not a citizen. Right now you're in Mexico."

CHAPTER LV

KIDNAPPED

MEXICO. Steve had never been to Mexico. Steve had never even been out of the country, so the news that he had just unintentionally traveled abroad would have been exciting, if he hadn't also unintentionally gotten himself kidnapped.

Although maybe he wasn't kidnapped. After all, Chuy hadn't said he was kidnapped, and he wasn't tied up in ropes or anything.

"Mexico!" Steve said. "I'm supposed to be in San Diego. It's very important that I return as soon as possible. I'm giving a talk tomorrow at the Model UN on cod fishing rights in Iceland. I better get back up to the U.S."

Chuy shook his head. "Sorry, *guey*. You can't leave."

"Chuy. Just let me go. I'll find my way back home. And I promise I won't even tell the cops in California." Steve *would* tell the cops in Mexico, though, who he was pretty sure were called *federales*.

"You gotta stay," Chuy said.

"But that's kidnapping," Steve said. "That has to be illegal here, too."

Chuy did not react.

"So what are you going to do with me?" Steve asked.

Chuy shrugged. "I don't know. That's up to her." He nodded over Steve's shoulder.

"Who?" Steve said, turning around.

Standing a few feet in front of the Packard, with an amused smile on her maybe beautiful face, was Alice Vanderdraak.

CHAPTER LVI

A LOVE STORY

"WAIT, WHAT?" said Steve.

"Hello, Steven," said Mrs. Vanderdraak.

"Steve," said Steve. "*You're* stealing the cars?"

Still, that smile.

"But," said Steve, "they're your cars. You own them with Mr. Vanderdraak."

The smile disappeared. "Please. You heard the way J. Nicholas talks. On and on about 'his collection.' Imagine twenty-five years of hearing about *his collection*." She paused. "It wasn't as bad when we first married, mind you. J. Nicholas was fun then. Even the cars were fun. He'd take me out driving down the coast, from his pied-à-terre in San Francisco down here to his Baja estate. He drove quite fast. And back then he'd let me drive. But back then I always felt like he was paying more attention to me than the cars. That changed."

Steve didn't know what to say or even how to arrange his face during this story. He looked at Chuy, who was looking at the Phoebus.

"You probably think I'm ridiculous," Mrs. Vanderdraak said. "A woman jealous of machines. But you wouldn't understand what it's like to be in a marriage like mine. How old are you?"

"Twelve."

"Twelve. You probably haven't even had a girlfriend yet."

"So?" Steve said. What did that have to do with anything? Steve didn't think he'd ever understand a marriage like this.

"Well," said Mrs. Vanderdraak, "you stop feeling like you even exist. I didn't grow up with money, and as a girl I dreamed of being fabulously rich. But being fabulously rich can be fabulously lonely. When J. talks about cars, I feel like I'm not even in the room. And nowadays he does nothing but talk about cars."

"So why steal them?" Steve asked. "Why not just tell him what's bothering you?"

Mrs. Vanderdraak laughed. "Talk to me when you've been married for twenty-five years."

Steve hated when people said things like that.

"When he got the Shelby," Mrs. Vanderdraak said, "that's when things got bad. He loved that car—spent all day with it, then talked about it all through dinner. It grew tiresome, then infuriating. If he loved the car so much, why didn't he marry it?"

Steve hadn't heard that joke since second grade.

"I fantasized about the car getting rear-ended at a traffic stop. Or better yet stolen. And then I realized: I could just steal it myself. At first just the idea was enough to give me pleasure and get me through another dinner. But then I began thinking about how I could actually do it. And so I paid Chuy—"

Chuy nodded bashfully.

"—to take it one night. Chuy had full access to J.'s garage, and J. trusted him completely. It was too easy, right, Chuy?"

"Sure," Chuy said.

"J. was morose! Every day he moped around the estate I was secretly jubilant. Then he bought the 2CV. And he fell in love with a car all over again."

"So you stole it," Steve said.

"Yes," said Mrs. Vanderdraak. "And now here's the sixth car I've stolen. The Packard Phoebus blah blah.

If J. only knew they were still right here on our estate."

"What?" Steve asked.

"Oh, yes. The property is huge. We own fifty acres down here. I don't know what this building used to be—some sort of wine cellar, I think—but I had it retrofitted years ago to store all my new cars."

"Wow," Steve said. It was all he could muster.

Mrs. Vanderdraak giggled. "You look so surprised. On the train, I was so worried when I found out you were a private investigator. I thought you'd figure out everything, spoil my whole plan. But I guess I didn't need to be, *detective*."

Steve's face grew red. "Excuse me, but I snuck into your hideout and then got you to confess all your crimes—that's pretty good detective work." Steve considered what she'd said about being worried about him on the train. *Wait!* "You were the one who tried to kill me in the sauna!" Steve said. "I escaped that!"

Mrs. Vanderdraak's face grew serious. "Oh no. Not kill you, Steve. I had timed everything so that when I came in to get you, you would just be badly burned."

That sounded even worse. This woman was a maniac.

"In the hospital you'd be out of my way." She shrugged.

"But wait," Steve said. "You were in the observation room, so how could you trap me in there . . . ?" He turned to Chuy.

Chuy smiled sheepishly.

So Chuy had been holding the door to the sauna closed. Steve was supposed to end up in the hospital, but he ended up surprising Chuy in the vault before he could change back into his mechanics' outfit.

"How could you, Chuy?" Steve said. He'd seemed like such a nice guy.

Chuy shrugged. "It's just a job, *guey.*" But he didn't look like he believed it. "Anyways—"

"Anyway," said Steve.

"What?" said Chuy.

"It's just 'anyway.'"

"Anyway," said Chuy, looking strangely at Steve, "what do you want me to do with him, *señora*?"

Mrs. Vanderdraak looked at her watch. "It's getting late. I may as well get some sleep tonight. We'll figure out what to do with him tomorrow."

It was time to fall back on his original plan. Steve held his magnifying glass aloft and aimed it at the Phoebus. Chuy looked concerned.

"Nobody better touch me," Steve said. "Either one of you makes one move, I'll throw this magnifying glass and break one of the car's windows or dent it or something." Steve wished he'd stopped at "throw this magnifying glass."

Mrs. Vanderdraak laughed. "Please do. I couldn't care less. I'll probably end up burning all these cars someday anyway."

Steve's right arm fell. Chuy quickly pinned both Steve's hands behind his back.

"Where do I put him?"

She motioned to a red door on the wall behind her. "Leave him in there with the other one."

CHAPTER LVII

A REUNION

STEVE WAS TOSSED into a small wood-paneled room with a desk and a chair. A single bulb dangled from a wire. Sitting in the chair was Claire Marriner.

"Steve!" Claire said. She was reading a different book.

"Hey, Claire," said Steve. He was glad to see a friend. Was Claire his friend? He hadn't known her very long, but she felt like a friend. Because what else would she be? Definitely not more than a friend. Yes. Steve was glad to see a friend.

The door to the room shut, and a lock clicked.

And Claire looked glad to see him, too. That was

good. It seemed like she wasn't mad at him anymore. Steve hoped she wouldn't bring up Cy.

"So," said Claire, "looks like you were wrong about my uncle, huh?"

Great.

"Maybe," Steve said.

"Maybe?" said Claire.

"Well, right now the evidence is pointing elsewhere."

"Typical," Claire said. "You can't admit that you were wrong."

Steve started a lap around the tiny room. Claire swiveled in her chair and glared at him. "Well," said Steve, "it wasn't him in the mask. But he was acting very suspicious. I mean, he kept disappearing. And you don't know this, but I followed him, and he threatened me. He said he was onto me, and that I would never prove anything. I mean, I know you don't want to believe this, Claire, but he could still be involved."

Claire's chair stopped rotating. "Steve," she said.

Steve stopped walking. "What?"

She was looking a little past him. "Steve. He was going to the café car. Sometimes my uncle drinks too much. Especially when he's on a job."

"Oh," Steve said. He was very uncomfortable, and suddenly the tiny room seemed even tinier.

"He's gotten in trouble for it before," Claire said. "Drinking. Almost got his license suspended. He hasn't had a job for a while. He was so excited when the Vanderdraaks got in touch. It's probably why he didn't see it coming."

"See what coming?" Steve said.

"The frame," Claire said. "Uncle Cy was in a frame. That's why I'm not mad at you anymore, Steve. You were supposed to think Cy was going to steal the car. Mrs. Vanderdraak set him up."

"What?" said Steve. "Where is he now?"

Claire looked impatient. "He got arrested back in San Diego. Right after the car got stolen, it was chaos. Mr. Vanderdraak weeping, Mrs. Vanderdraak comforting him. Then the cops came and arrested my uncle. I guess they caught that car thief nearby—the one with the beard, only he'd shaved it—and he told the cops that Uncle Cy was his partner, the inside man. Cy denied it, but they had some security footage of the two of them talking in the train station—Uncle Cy swears the guy was just asking him if he knew what the weather would be tomorrow. But nobody believed him. Except me.

"I was already suspicious before we got to San Diego. After I left you on the train and went back to the Vanderdraaks' car, I noticed that Chuy was left-handed. And he disappeared as soon as we got to San Diego. And then the Phoebus was stolen while the Medea was being disconnected from the Sunset Coastliner. And Chuy never came back. They asked me a bunch of questions about my uncle at the police station, but I told them they should be trying to find Chuy. I told the police about everything that happened on the train. But they thought I was crazy. I could see it in their faces.

"And then I guess they told Mrs. Vanderdraak, who laughed and gave Chuy an alibi and told them she and her husband would take care of me until the situation with Uncle Cy was sorted out. Apparently Uncle Cy agreed, which pretty soon turned out to be a dumb move. Mrs. Vanderdraak drove me down here. She was nice in the car— Mr. Vanderdraak stayed up in San Diego to deal with the police—and I told her I thought my uncle had been framed and that Chuy was the real thief. When we got to their estate, she told me I was causing a lot of trouble and locked me in this room. I heard her saying to Chuy that she was going to tell the police I ran away."

Steve felt mad at himself. How had he missed all this? And also mad at Mrs. Vanderdraak, mostly for choosing to frame Cy instead of Steve.

"So how'd you get down to Mexico?" Claire said. "When did you figure out that Mrs. Vanderdraak was stealing the cars? Were you following us? And did you tell the police before you left California?"

"Uh," said Steve. "I just figured out about Mrs. Vanderdraak about five minutes ago."

"What?" said Claire. "Then how did you get here?"

"I got stolen with the Phoebus."

"What?"

"Have you ever heard of the Wooden Horse?" Steve asked.

"No."

"It's an old private detective's trick. Basically, I realized the best way to figure out who was stealing the cars was to hide in the Phoebus. Then the plan was to bust out once I was inside the thieves' secret lair."

"Oh, like the Trojan horse."

"No, this is called the Wooden Horse."

Claire shook her head quickly. "Where did you hide?"

"In the trunk."

"Wait, what?"

"In the trunk of the car."

"But you can't open a trunk from the inside."

"I know that *now*."

"Everybody knows that, Steve. Toddlers know

that. There are, like, a million stories on the local news about how dangerous it is when kids lock themselves in trunks."

"Okay, well, I don't watch the local news."

"Unless you're on it," Claire said, rolling her eyes.

"I *was* on the news," Steve said.

"Well, now you can be on it again. Tonight at seven: Don't let your toddler or private detective lock himself in a trunk."

Steve ignored her. He looked up at the ceiling.

"What are you doing?" Claire asked.

"Trying to find a way out of here."

"There's no way out. I checked. I've already been in here a couple hours."

Steve continued his examination of the ceiling and four walls around him. Claire was right.

"So now what?" Claire asked.

"Well, now we wait for Chuy to come back in here, and we fight our way out."

"You mean kayo our way to freedom?" Claire smirked.

"That's right."

"Steve. We're twelve."

"So what? I kayoed a guy once." *With Dana's help,* he thought. "Here's the plan. When we hear someone coming, you unscrew the lightbulb. That way Chuy won't be able to see. Then I'll throw a haymaker."

Claire looked skeptical. "Okay. What do we do until then?"

"I don't know."

Steve turned his head toward the door.

Someone was inserting a key into the lock!

CHAPTER LVIII

AMBUSH!

CLAIRE SPRANG ONTO THE DESK. Steve positioned himself next to the door.

"Ouch!" Claire said. "I burned my fingers."

The doorknob turned but did not open.

"Use my sweatshirt to cover your hands," Steve said, pulling his blue hoodie over his head and tossing it to Claire.

The sound of another key.

The lights went out.

"Got it!" Claire said.

In the dark, glass shattered.

"I dropped the bulb!"

Steve and Claire prepared their attack.

"Shhh!" said Steve.

Steve heard the doorknob turn.

Steve put his fist up next to his right ear.

The door's hinges squeaked.

Steve swung wide and hard.

His fist flew through the dark.

The punch landed!

CHAPTER LIX

THE WAY OF THE WIZARD

"Ouch," said a familiar voice.

"Dana?" said Steve.

"Ow," said Dana. "What the—what was that, Steve?"

"Dana?" said Steve.

"Yeah. You know it's me. Why did you punch me?"

"I thought you were Chuy! Claire, it's Dana!"

"I can hear that," said Claire.

"Dana!" Steve shouted. He did a small dance that nobody would ever see. "How did you get here?"

"I was in the backseat of the Phoebus."

"What?"

"Well, I thought about why the Hound with Two Tails didn't work—you know, because you kept looking back at me because you knew I was coming?"

"Yeah," Steve said quickly. He wished Claire weren't around to hear this.

"And then I thought about how in the second Wizards' Worlds book, *The Alabaster Scramaseax*, there's this apprentice, Drakkar, who has to go on this quest, and his adept, Nywylly, makes herself invisible and accompanies him, and she doesn't even tell Drakkar, because she figures that if Drakkar knows that she is there helping him—"

"Does it have to be all wizards all the time with you?" Steve said.

"Anyway, I got in the backseat and hid under that sheet so I could back you up without any danger."

"Ace! The Wooden Hound with Two Tails!" said Steve.

"Yeah," said Dana. "Pretty much."

"All right," said Claire. "Let's get out of here."

CHAPTER LX

ESCAPE!

THE THREE KIDS stood in the middle of the warehouse. The moon, visible through skylights, faintly illuminated the building. "Okay," said Steve, "here's the plan." He pointed to an aluminum loading door. "Dana, you see about opening that door. Claire and I will try to find the keys to one of these cars."

"There's a big board with a bunch of keys over there," Dana said, pointing behind Steve. "That's where I got these." He held up the ring of keys he'd used to break them out a couple minutes earlier.

"Good," said Steve. "We'll drive out of here and find some *federales*. Let's go."

Dana ran over to the loading door, Steve and Claire to the wall of keys.

There were six sets of keys hanging from six hooks. It looked like each set was labeled, but Steve couldn't read the writing in the dark. He put his nose right up against the wall so he could see better.

"Do you even know how to drive?" Claire asked.

"Yeah," said Steve. "I'm really good."

"Cool."

It was too dark to read. Steve grabbed all six key rings. "Come on," he said.

They sprinted over to the Tucker Torpedo, which sat in a pool of moonlight on the warehouse floor.

The door was unlocked. Steve sat in the driver's seat and rested his hands on the wheel. So this was how the Bailey Brothers felt. Except they were always speeding along the open highway, engine purring, blond or brown hair blowing in the wind—which was exactly what Steve would be doing soon.

Claire got in the seat next to Steve.

"Are you going to start her up?" she asked.

Steve fumbled with the keys. "Here." He handed five sets to Claire. "Hold these."

He tried to insert the keys on the first ring. Neither fit in the ignition. He threw the keys out of the car.

"Give me some more keys," Steve said, holding out his hand.

"How about 'please'?" Claire said.

"Hurry, please," said Steve.

Claire slapped another set in his hand.

Nope.

A key on the third ring fit.

"Here we go," Steve said.

He turned the key.

The engine did not start.

Steve tried again. There was nothing. No sound. Not even the electric click of a dead battery. Steve tried the remaining keys. None fit.

"There's something wrong with the engine," Steve said.

"Pop the hood," said Claire.

"Do you know how to fix cars?"

"A little. My uncle taught me." Claire got out of the sedan.

It took Steve a while to find the right latch.

Claire disappeared underneath the hood.

She came around to Steve's side of the car. "This car is a fake."

CHAPTER LXI

COUNTERFEIT!

"No WAY," said Steve. The Tucker looked just like the one in the Bailey Brothers books.

"Seriously," said Claire. "Everything under the hood is just there for decoration."

"How can you tell?" said Steve. He was beginning to wonder if she actually knew about cars.

"Well," said Claire, "probably the easiest way to explain it to someone who doesn't understand cars is that the engine says Mazda on it."

Steve hopped out of the driver's seat and looked under the hood.

Claire pointed. It was unmistakable. There, visible

in the silver light, was MAZDA and a bunch of numbers.

"Nothing here is really connected, either," Claire said. "This engine won't start."

Why would Mr. Vanderdraak buy a counterfeit Tucker?

Dana, breathless, came up behind them.

"I can't open the door," he said. "I think I found a control box, but there's a keypad with a bunch of numbers, and I think you have to know a code."

"This car doesn't start anyway," Steve said. He slammed down the hood. "It's a fake."

"What?" Dana said.

"I know," said Steve.

"So what do we do?" Claire asked.

"We can try to start some of these other cars," Steve said. "But if we can't open that loading door, there's not much point."

"So we're trapped," Claire said.

Steve starting walking in a tight figure eight, thinking.

"Shhh," said Dana. "Do you hear that?"

All three kids got quiet. It was the sound of an engine—a big one—getting closer fast.

"It sounds like a truck," Claire said.

"It's coming toward us," said Dana.

The truck pulled up outside the building and stopped.

For almost a minute everything was quiet. Nobody moved.

Then Steve heard the doors open and close. Men shouted to each other. Metal ground against metal.

"Okay," Steve said. "They're going to be coming inside here."

"What do we do?" Dana asked.

Before Steve could say anything, the loading door groaned and began to roll open.

CHAPTER LXII

THE WOODEN HORSE, TAKE TWO

THE LOADING DOOR was maybe twenty-five yards away from the Tucker. Steve, Claire, and Dana ducked behind the car. Outside, ground lights along a narrow road lit up a large delivery truck. The back of the truck was open, and inside was a black 1932 Packard Twin Six Sport Phoebus.

"I don't get it," Dana said. "I thought the other one was in Rhode Island."

Chuy appeared at the back of the truck and began lowering a metal ramp. He shouted orders to two other men in Spanish.

A second Phoebus. The fake Tucker. Seven cars

but only six sets of keys on the wall. Something in Steve's mind snapped into place. "We need to get in the Phoebus," he whispered.

"What?" Claire said.

"Wooden Horse, take two," Steve said. "They're going to steal the Phoebus right now. That's our ticket out."

"I'm not getting in the trunk of a car," Claire said.

"Not the trunk. The backseat. Come on." The men were pushing the second Phoebus down the ramp.

Steve led the way as they raced across the warehouse floor, keeping to the shadows. They reached the car. The lamps came on. Yellow light flooded the room.

"Hurry," Steve whispered. He gently opened the driver-side door. It clicked softly. Dana got in first, then Claire. They disappeared under the white cloth in the backseat. Steve got in last. Softly shutting the door behind him, he pulled the sheet over his head.

They all made themselves as small as they could, packed into the backseat of the Packard. Steve slid his arms under the driver's seat. Claire did too. It was hot under the sheet, and hard to breathe, but something smelled like watermelons. Steve figured it was Claire.

Steve listened to the men's voices, to loud thuds and occasional clangs. They lay huddled there awhile.

Steve's legs began cramping. He wondered whether he was right—were these men not going to steal the Phoebus after all? Claire fidgeted a bit next to him. Steve elbowed her to tell her not to move. She elbowed him back. Annoying.

The driver's door opened. Steve froze. He felt Claire tense next to him. Someone sat in the driver's seat—the cushion sagged, and Steve felt the weight against his forearms. He did not move.

The Phoebus started. Its tires squeaked on the cement floor. They were moving.

CHAPTER LXIII

STOWAWAYS

THEY DROVE FOR A WHILE on what felt like winding roads. Steve was thrown against Claire, then Claire against Steve. Steve couldn't decide whether he'd rather be next to Claire or have more room, like Dana. They drove for more than twenty-five minutes before the car's horn honked twice and stopped. The engine was still running. There was the sound of a large metal door opening, and the car drove inside a building.

The car stopped. The engine died. The driver exited the Packard. There was the sound of receding footsteps, and then of the big door clanging shut.

All was quiet. Still Steve didn't move. Neither did anyone else.

For ten minutes they lay huddled in the backseat of the Phoebus. Then Steve whispered, "Okay."

They tore the sheet off themselves. Steve took a deep breath of cool air. He looked around.

"Déjà vu," Dana said.

They were in a small warehouse surrounded by six beautiful old cars. At first the setup seemed almost identical to the last building, but there were differences. The upper halves of three of the walls here were large glass windows. Through them Steve could see palm fronds blowing softly in a breeze. There was another difference that boosted Steve's heart rate: In addition to a metal loading door, there was a regular wooden door on the windowless wall.

"Come on," said Steve. He dashed toward the door. They would have to risk setting out on foot.

Steve, Claire, and Dana gathered in front of the door.

"Wait. What's going on?" Claire asked. "What is this place?"

"Someone has been stealing Mrs. Vanderdraak's cars and replacing them with fakes. This is where the real ones are."

"Why? Who would do that?" Claire asked.

Steve grabbed the door handle. He turned and smiled at Claire. "Who do you think? Mr. Vanderdraak."

"Why?" Dana asked.

Steve sighed. "I'll explain later. We've got to get out of here first."

He opened the door.

They were bathed in the high beams of a car parked just outside.

"Well, well, well," said Mr. Vanderdraak.

CHAPTER LXIV

TROUBLE ON THE BEACH

"THIS IS PERFECT TIMING, ISN'T IT, CHUY?"

The two men got out of the car. Steve squinted. It appeared to be a lime-green dune buggy.

"I was just coming by to see the latest addition to my collection. Chuy, you didn't tell me we had guests."

"I didn't know they were here, *jefe*," Chuy said, surprised. Steve shielded his eyes with his hands—he wanted to see Chuy's face.

"Here," said Mr. Vanderdraak, leaning into the buggy and turning off the headlights. "That's better."

In the moonlight Steve saw that they had exited onto a beach. The buggy was parked on a sandy road that curved and ran uphill to their left. On their right the surf broke gently on the shore.

"Now, children, it's delightful to see you again."

"Don't play nice, Mr. Vanderdraak," said Steve. "We know what you're up to."

"We do?" Dana said.

Mr. Vanderdraak laughed. "What am I up to?"

"You know your wife has been stealing your cars, so you're stealing them back."

Mr. Vanderdraak's smile disappeared. "Well, I guess you do know what I'm up to."

"That's right," Dana said.

"But here's what I don't get," Steve said. "Why go through all this trouble? Why not just report your wife to the police?"

"Then she'd go to jail," Mr. Vanderdraak said.

"And the insurance money," Claire said.

"What?" Steve asked.

"The insurance company made him hire my uncle," Claire said. "He's basically getting these cars for free."

Mr. Vanderdraak smiled. "A clever girl," he said.

"So you don't care about your wife going to jail at all," Dana said.

"Oh no. I do care. That wouldn't be any fun," said Mr. Vanderdraak.

"Fun?" said Steve.

"Oh, yes. Fun: Alice thinks she has one up on me, but of course I have one up on her. She doesn't realize that Chuy came to me as soon as she proposed he steal my Shelby. And so I hatched this plan: I had Chuy make a replica of the car—he's very good with bodywork—and we swapped the real thing for an ersatz version. You should have seen her when she pretended to console me: I could see she was just reveling in outsmarting me. I'll admit, it was hard pretending to be maudlin when I was enjoying myself so much. You have no idea how fun it is, watching her think she has everything figured out. That's why I invited you onto the Medea—to watch her squirm while her perfect plan was disrupted."

"But you guys are crazy," Claire said. "I mean, what if she figures out you're stealing the cars back from her?"

"Oh no," said Mr. Vanderdraak. "She doesn't have any idea where this warehouse is. Our estate is huge."

"But that's exactly what she said about her warehouse, and you!" said Claire. "This could go on forever."

Mr. Vanderdraak looked momentarily concerned. "Hmm," he said. "No, I don't think so."

"I really don't see why you two don't just talk about these cars," Steve said.

"You've never had a girlfriend, have you, Steve?" Mr. Vanderdraak asked.

"He hasn't," Dana said.

"Why does everyone keep saying that? I think I have a good point!"

"Me too," Claire muttered.

"I mean, wouldn't that be better than committing all these crimes?"

"Crimes?" said Mr. Vanderdraak. "What crimes? My wife and I both own the cars. We're just moving our property back and forth across the estate."

"What crimes? Are you joking me?" Steve said. "Insurance fraud. Framing Claire's uncle. Trying to burn me in the sauna. Assault with a lead pipe. Kidnapping two kids. All of you are going to jail."

"Two kids?" asked Mr. Vanderdraak. "There are three of you."

"Yeah, your wife only kidnapped Steve and Claire," Dana said. "I snuck down here."

"Well," said Mr. Vanderdraak, "we'll have to make it three now. Chuy, you grab the boys."

CHAPTER LXV

SEASIDE SET-TO

WHAT HAPPENED NEXT HAPPENED FAST.

Mr. Vanderdraak lunged for Claire, who reached up and grabbed him by the ears. She pulled down hard. Vanderdraak howled. As he doubled over, Claire kneed him hard in the solar plexus.

Steve watched, captivated, and so forgot about Chuy until the big man was lifting him off the ground. His arms pinned in Chuy's bear hug, Steve kicked—mightily, but pointlessly.

But then Chuy stumbled, and now Dana was on his back, grabbing a handful of Chuy's hair. Chuy shouted, and Steve didn't need to know Spanish to know Chuy was not happy. Steve kept kicking and wriggling like a caught salmon. Dana dug his knees into Chuy's side. The mechanic stumbled for what seemed like yards, reaching back to swat at Dana with his left hand. Steve struggled but still could not get free.

And then Claire was there, below Steve, pulling on Chuy's right arm.

"Stop kicking for a second, Steve!" she said.

She grabbed Steve's legs and yanked down on them hard. Steve felt his knees pop; then, freed from the man's grasp, he fell a few feet, face-first into sand.

Chuy, with both arms free now, reached for Dana. Steve pushed himself up and, teeth grinding on sand, kicked him in the shin. Chuy swiped at Steve, who dove for the ground, and Dana took the opportunity to spring off Chuy's back.

Steve watched his chum take off down the sand. Chuy looked down at Steve and then turned to chase Dana instead.

Steve rolled over, relieved, and turned to see Mr. Vanderdraak coming up behind Claire. He reached with his right hand, digging his fingers deep into the beach, and flung a fistful of sand up at Vanderdraak's face.

Claire saw the sand coming and started to duck,

but it was no use. The sand spread everywhere as it flew through the air, and a lot of it ended up in Claire's face. Steve felt bad about that, but Mr. Vanderdraak was reeling backward, wiping his eyes. Steve stood up, ready to charge him.

And then there was a terrible noise, an explosion, and the sound of shattering glass.

CHAPTER LXVI

DESTRUCTO

STEVE BRIXTON LOOKED UP from where he lay on the beach, his hands still covering his head.

Through the glass walls of the warehouse he saw orange and black flames licking at the building's ceiling. The whole thing flickered. The smell of gasoline was all around, and Steve's throat burned.

Mr. Vanderdraak stood facing the warehouse, stunned, slowly rubbing at his eyes with his right hand.

Chuy came running up the beach behind Steve. Steve watched him throw the door to the warehouse open, disappear inside, and then come out, seconds later, coughing.

"She burned them!" he shouted. "She blew them up." He dropped to his knees, coughed some more, and shook his head. *"Estos maridos están locos,"* he said.

Mr. Vanderdraak still stood there.

Then Dana was pulling on Steve.

"Come on, come on," he said. "Let's go. Before they remember we're here."

Steve felt like he was just waking up. He stumbled to his feet. Claire was there beside him too. He shook his head to clear it.

"Follow me," Steve said. He flew off in a straight line toward the ocean, stopping when a wave broke over his ankles. "Stay in the water," he told Claire and Dana. "It will hide our footprints."

Now, north or south? Steve's first instinct was to go north, toward California. But then that's probably exactly what they'd expect him to do. So south. Unless they figured he'd know they'd think he'd go north. In which case he should go south. Unless . . .

Steve felt like his brain was folding in on itself. He was thinking like the Vanderdraaks. He needed to make a decision. To trust his gut.

South.

"This way," he said. They ran.

Steve took one last look over his shoulder, back up

The trio escaped while the warehouse burned.

the beach. Silhouetted against the flames in the warehouse's doorway were a man and a woman—Mr. and Mrs. Vanderdraak. From where Steve was, it looked like they were holding hands.

CHAPTER LXVII

A FINAL RIDDLE

DANA LED THE WAY, followed by Claire, then Steve. It was hard running. Steve's feet sank deep every time they hit the sand, and every few seconds a wave would catch him around the calves. His wet socks squished inside his shoes. Soon Steve was out of breath.

Steve paused, hands on knees, then started up again. His chest hurt. His right side radiated pain. He couldn't let them get too far ahead.

This was bad. They were hemmed in—the ocean on the right and sheer cliffs to the left. If the Vanderdraaks came after them in the dune buggy, there'd be no place to hide. Steve kept checking for a break in the rocks, or even a place that wasn't too steep to climb. But there were only tall palm trees with bushy trunks that looked like fur, and behind those the cliff side rising up into blackness.

They needed to get off this beach as soon as possible. But there was no way out.

Maybe they should have gone north. It was too late to turn back now.

The group slowed down to a jog, and then a walk. After a while Steve noticed that birds had begun singing in the brush beside the beach. The sky, still mostly black, was beginning to glow. Soon the sun would rise. They'd be spotted easily in the daylight.

Dana and Claire stopped. Steve caught up.

"Where are we going?" Dana said.

"I don't know," said Steve. "But we've got to put as much distance between us and them as we can."

"We could get lost and die out here," Dana said.

Steve shook his head. They'd be caught first. "Let's just keep going," he said. "As soon as we see a way off this beach, we take it."

Claire nodded.

It was windier now, blowing offshore. The palm trees rustled noisily. Out to their right, tall waves broke in a long clear line.

"I need to take a break," Claire said. Steve was grateful. He was exhausted.

A faint, lonely cry came from some rocks jutting out in the water.

Steve looked out to sea. "Is that some kind of bird?"

"I think it's just the rocks," Dana said. "That happens sometimes—there are holes in the rocks like a flute."

They stood in the water, listening to the sound.

"It's a perfect C," Claire said.

Steve registered her sentence. He took a sharp breath. "What?"

"The note the rocks are making. It's a perfect C."

Steve chewed his thumbnail. He smiled, then started walking in a circle.

"What?" Claire said.

Steve was reaching in the pocket of his cargo shorts and pulling out his notebook.

He flipped through it.

"Uh-oh," Dana said. "Guys. Headlights." Steve turned around. Far down the shore, two yellow circles were coming down the beach. It was the dune buggy.

"Let's get moving," Dana said. "Find someplace to hide."

"Hold on," Steve said. "Wait."

He was looking in his notebook again.

"Are you crazy?"

Steve opened to some notes he'd made last Wednesday night. He lit up the face of his calculator watch so he could read the page.

Turn west at the south pole,

    go down, then climb over the

old man who sleeps on the beach.

   Turn right and then walk

      to the place where the

        sea sings its own name.

"The sea is singing its own name," Steve said. "C. Sea. I think this might be Danimal's secret spot."

"What's a Danimal?" Claire asked.

"What are you talking about, Steve?" said Dana.

"Guys," said Steve. "I think I can get us out of here. We just need to reverse the directions."

"What directions?"

"His grandfather's directions. We should keep going down the beach."

"I really think we should find somewhere to hide," Dana said.

"Look around," Steve said. "There's nowhere to hide.

Their only hope lay in the darkness ahead.

We're totally exposed out here. Trapped."

The headlights were getting closer. The buggy's engine was now audible in the distance.

"Come on," said Steve. "Let's run a little farther. I think the old man who sleeps on the beach might be up there."

"What does that even mean?" Dana said.

"I have no idea!" said Steve, sprinting down the shore.

Steve ran, not knowing how long he needed to run or what he was looking for. But his stomach cramp had been replaced by the warm glow of a hunch. He hoped he was right: This could be the lucky break that made a good sleuth a great sleuth.

"They're getting closer," Claire yelled from behind Steve.

The engine was louder now, but Steve didn't look back. His eyes were focused forward, looking for the old man. The sky was gray, and it was getting easier to see. That was good for Steve, but also good for the Vanderdraaks.

"Steve!" shouted Dana. He didn't say anything else. He didn't need to. Dana was not happy with this plan. Steve kept running.

Then, suddenly, Steve stopped.

"There," he said.

He pointed to a large rock that abutted the cliff side.

"What?" said Dana.

"The old man who sleeps on the beach!"

"That's a rock," Dana said.

"Yeah, but it looks like an old man lying on his back. See, there are his feet. There's his beard, and there's his nose."

"I don't see it," Dana said.

"I guess I kind of see it," Claire said.

"See?" said Steve.

"I think it looks more like a dragon's head," Dana said.

"Oh, come on. A dragon? Are you serious with this?"

"Oh, I kind of see the dragon," Claire said. "Like, there's his snout."

"Yeah," said Dana.

Steve looked behind him. He could see a greenish dot now. Soon—very soon—the Vanderdraaks would be close enough to spot them.

"I'm going for it," Steve said.

He ran up toward the rock.

Claire followed.

Dana came up last, walking backward, brushing the sand with his arm to cover up their tracks.

Steve stood atop the old man's belly and grinned.

At his feet was a crack in the cliff, just wide enough for a grown man to fit through. "Follow me," he said.

"Down there?" said Claire. "I can't see the bottom."

"There's a secret path down there," said Steve.

"I don't think it's a good idea to jump down a hole in a cliff," Dana said. "What if it's a sea cave?"

"It's not a sea cave," Steve said.

"It could be a sea cave," said Dana.

The buggy's engine grew louder.

Steve jumped into the blackness.

CHAPTER LXVIII

UP THE ARROYO

HE LANDED ON SOFT SAND.

"Not a sea cave," he called up.

Claire hopped down after him. Dana slid down.

"Wait," Steve said.

They pressed their backs against the smooth stone and heard the buggy's motor come close. Steve stopped breathing for as long as he could. The buggy passed them by. The sound of its engine grew distant.

Steve clapped his hands.

He had saved everybody.

Claire hugged Steve.

Steve looked over her shoulder at Dana, whose eyes were wide.

"Let's get moving," Steve said.

The narrow ravine opened into an arroyo that they followed up a hill a long way. The arroyo became a path that dumped them out on a two-lane highway next to a long-closed roadside concession stand. Painted on the side of the old wooden building was a peeling advertisement that showed three penguins cradling ice cream bars in their wings while they danced around a barber's pole. Across the top of the painting were the words ES TIEMPO DE HELADOS in snow-capped letters.

"The south pole," Steve said, putting his notebook back in his pocket.

"What?" said Dana.

They started down the highway together.

CHAPTER LXIX:

THE START OF SOMETHING

STEVE HADN'T SLEPT since his naps in the Phoebus's trunk, so that day passed like a dream: trudging along the road underneath sky that went from orange to blue; catching a ride on the back of a truck filled with ripe tomatoes; arriving in a small seaside town of wooden shacks and brightly painted adobe buildings; finding the local police station; Dana talking, in Spanish, to a police officer with deep laugh lines on his face; Claire reading a beat-up English paperback the cop pulled from a desk drawer; phone calls, long waits, and tacos and cold horchata for lunch; and then, before sunset, the arrival in handcuffs of the Vanderdraaks and Chuy; more statements, more translating; that evening, a small caravan of trucks and cars pulling up bearing *federales*, American officials, and Rick (Rick was the only person wearing a bullet-proof vest); a long drive home during which Dana learned that the Model UN had voted, in the absence of a speech from the Icelandic delegation, to award Great Britain unrestricted fishing rights to the waters off Iceland, and Steve learned, talking to his mom on Rick's cell phone, that he was grounded.

But there was one moment among that day's otherwise hazy parade of events that would remain clear and vivid in Steve's memory for the rest of his life.

It happened just after lunch. Steve was standing near the police station watching two surfers who'd paddled out past the waves. Their brown backs were to the shore, and they sat half submerged on their boards, watching for the next swell to come rolling in. They reminded Steve of Danimal. He wondered where Danimal was, and if he'd gone to the police to report that fake shark attack. When Steve got back to Ocean Park, he'd have to find him and tell him he'd found his grandfather's secret spot. Steve guessed that meant he would come out of retirement, at least for now, and the thought of his future cases made him happy. Of course, those same cases, like his next case,

Danger Goes Berserk, would bring about their share of danger too.

Twelve years old was too young to retire, Steve decided. He thought about what Mrs. Vanderdraak had said to him about talking to her later, when he'd been married for twenty-five years. Marriage was a mystery Steve had no interest in solving. The Vanderdraaks were incomprehensible to him. He had learned so many of their secrets and had only come away more confused. What bound them together? It didn't seem healthy. Why was his mom with Rick, for that matter, when Rick was a doofus and his mom was not? Or Dana and Other Dana. What was going on there? No, Steve decided, he'd never understand what Mrs. Vanderdraak had been talking about, because he wanted nothing to do with love.

"Hey, Steve," Dana said behind him. Dana had both hands in his pockets and looked nervous. Steve figured it was time to go give another statement to the police officer.

"So, well, you know Claire—I mean, of course you know her; we both know her—but um, she wanted me to ask you—"

Steve noticed now that Claire was standing under an arch on the patio of the little police station.

"—I mean," Dana said, "she was wondering if you wanted to be her boyfriend."

Steve felt like he had just taken a Shawn Bailey haymaker right to the kisser, but in a good way. Steve walked past Dana and up the brick path to where Claire was standing with her hands behind her back.

"Sure," Steve said.

Steve must don a neon wetsuit and get to work.
But with three cases going at once,
will Steve be in over his head?
Find out in:

BEGINNING AGAIN

STEVE BRIXTON, private detective, age twelve and freshly back from retirement, was reading in his office. Until last week, what was now Steve's office had been just a large doghouse in Steve Brixton's backyard, but the Brixtons did not own a dog and never had. The previous tenants had a Saint Bernard named Bandy, and when they'd moved away, they'd taken the dog but left the doghouse. Steve's mom had been using it for storage until Steve had convinced her that it was pretty much begging to be converted into the headquarters of a world-famous detective agency.

Steve had swept the place out and painted the

walls white. He'd hung up a map of Ocean Park and the surrounding coast, and he'd bought a small box of map tacks to help him keep track of crime waves. (Right now the map featured a single red pin, marking the location of the office in which the map now hung, but Steve was ready with more pins of many colors, just in case.) A small card table was Steve's desk. There were two tiny wooden chairs. In the evenings, light came from a lamp powered by a bright orange extension cord that ran across the backyard and up through Steve's bedroom window.

The space was a bit cramped, but it was clean and bright, and as long as you crouched, it could fit one comfortably—and up to two uncomfortably.

The best part: Steve had hired a professional sign painter to letter his name where the dog's name used to be—right above the door, or doorway, since there really wasn't a door, just a rectangular hole in the wall for a dog to enter and exit—and it looked like this:

And so, on a Thursday evening, Steve put his feet on his desk and read. Outside, the dark sky was shot through with peaches and pinks, and the office glowed in the dusk light. Steve's desk lamp was still unlit. He tilted back in his chair.

Behind Steve's head, on shelves he'd installed himself, were the shiny red spines of the books collectively known as the Bailey Brothers Mysteries. The Bailey Brothers Mysteries related the heart-pounding, rip-roaring adventures of Shawn and Kevin Bailey, teenage brothers, straight-A students, and red-blooded, corn-fed supersleuths. The books were by Steve's favorite author and mortal enemy, MacArthur Bart, a man who had turned to a life of crime after a long bout of writer's block. Steve had uncovered his hero's villainy when he'd discovered *The Ghostwriter Secret*—and although Steve had foiled one of Bart's schemes, the man had gotten away. It still bugged Steve that Bart was a free man. Even now Bart was no doubt incubating his sinister schemes in some dark and teeming fold of America's criminal underbelly.

Still, his books were pretty ace.

And the fact was this: Bart and the Bailey Brothers had taught Steve everything he knew about the art of detection. Steve had read and reread the fifty-eight

Bailey Brothers mysteries, plus he was deeply familiar with *The Bailey Brothers' Detective Handbook*. The handbook, which compiled the accumulated professional wisdom of Shawn and Kevin Bailey, was pretty much full-to-bursting with tricks and tips for gumshoes of all stripes. There were chapters like "Useful Morse Code" (... --- ... and -.-. .- -. -. .. -... .- .-.. ...) and "How to Outwit Hypnotists" (sing "The Star-Spangled Banner" backward).

Right now, the handbook was lying open on Steve's desk while he read Bailey Brothers #25: *The Clue of the Caves in the Cove*. The story was at a good part:

> Fair-haired Kevin Bailey opened up the throttle and expertly piloted the *Deducer VII* across the rough seas. "Keep an eye out for the *Dark and Stormy*! Her black hull will be hard to spot in this pea soup!" he shouted above the roar of the speedboat's motor.
>
> "Aye, aye!" cried dark-haired Shawn, who was manning the *Deducer VII*'s powerful search lamp. "Joseph Tanaka and his smugglers will never get away."
>
> Their stout chum, Ernest Plumly, was

looking green. "I shouldn't have eaten such a big lunch," he groaned. "I don't know if I can ever look at a roast beef sandwich again."

"Somebody write that down!" chuckled Shawn.

"If he keeps that pledge, Albert's Delicatessen will soon be out of business!" grinned Kevin.

"Don't bet on it, fellows," Ernest rejoined with a rueful smile. "I didn't say anything about ham sandwiches."

The boys all laughed.

"Scampering squirrels!" exclaimed eagle-eyed Shawn, pointing straight ahead. "There she is! The *Dark and Stormy!*"

The smugglers' ship emerged from the fog.

Kevin got on the *Deducer VII*'s bullhorn as he slowed the boat. "Give it up, Tanaka!" he warned. "Three Coast Guard cutters are right behind us."

The hatch of the criminals' craft opened up. Joseph Tanaka popped up and shrieked, "You don't have any evidence, Baileys!" Laughing, the swarthy ringleader dumped a wooden crate into the ocean!

Quick as a flash, Shawn Bailey, who was an excellent skin diver and proficient in aquatic lifesaving techniques, dove into the choppy waters. With a few powerful strokes, he made his way toward the *Dark and Stormy*, then disappeared beneath the swells.

Many tense seconds passed as Kevin and Ernest waited for the brave sleuth to resurface.

"Sure seems like he's been down there a while," Ernest worried.

"These are rougher seas than he's used to swimming," Kevin fretted.

Then, all of a sudden, Shawn Bailey's head broke the surface of the water. He was grinning and holding a clear bag. "Here's your evidence, Tanaka!" he exulted. He peered at the contents of the bag and read the label. "I happen to know that these are controlled pharmaceuticals! I overheard my doctor mention this particular type of medicine to a nurse last week, when I went in for my annual physical!"

"Blast you, Baileys!" Tanaka raged. The

smuggler's long black braid flapped behind him in the wind, and his gold earrings shone in the light of the *Deducer*'s lamp. "Too bad you'll never make it back to shore."

"What do you mean?" Kevin queried on the bullhorn. "The *Deducer VII*'s shipshape!"

"That may be so," snarled Tanaka, "but she's carrying a time bomb!"

Kevin and Ernest looked at each other in terror. *Suddenly the ticking noise they'd heard in the boathouse made sense!*

Steve turned the page just as a large figure blocked the doorway of the Brixton Brothers Detective Agency, plunging the office into darkness.

It was Danimal!

BOARD TROUBLE

"HEY, LITTLE MAN," said the big man in the doorway. Steve recognized him.

"Hi, Danimal," said Steve. "Come on in."

"New office, huh?" said Danimal, ducking through the entry. He was wearing shorts and a baggy tank top with a duck on it. His long hair was held back by sunglasses. Danimal looked around. "Place is pretty sick. Cramped, but sick. It could use a window, though."

"Well, the door's sort of the window," Steve said.

"Yeah, I guess. A real window would really open the place up, though."

"Yeah, well it used to be a doghouse."

"Right, right." Danimal looked uncomfortable, bent over at the waist and still pressed up against the ceiling.

Steve motioned for Danimal to sit. Danimal was too big for the chair. He folded his legs underneath him and sat on the floor.

"You can just put the chair outside," Steve said. It was taking up a lot of room.

"Good idea." Danimal pushed the chair through the doorway. It tipped over and fell on the lawn.

"So what's up?" Steve asked.

"I want to hire you, little man."

There wasn't room for Steve to put his feet up on the desk anymore. There was barely room for the desk. He opened up his black notebook and grabbed a pen. "What's the case?" he asked.

"Point Panic again." Point Panic was what everybody had been calling Mímulo Point, a nearby surf spot, ever since fins had been spotted offshore. Steve had first met Danimal in his last adventure, *It Happened on a Train*—the surfer had been attacked at Point Panic and his board chewed up. Steve had determined that the shark attack had been faked— although why someone would stage a bogus shark attack remained a mystery. Steve's fake-shark theory had been published in the local newspaper, and the point had recently been reopened, but lingering fear had kept the lineup sparse.

Danimal leaned forward. "So I check the surf report yesterday and I just know the point'll be going off. I strap a couple boards to the car and peel out. And as I turn the bend before Mímulo, the sun is coming up, and sure enough—corduroy out to the horizon."

Steve stopped taking notes and looked up.

"The swell," Danimal said. "Waves. Lots of them."

"Okay," said Steve.

"So I park out on the point, right behind this old ice cream truck painted like a leopard—which I already know is bad news."

"Why?"

"Truck belongs to the Berserkers. You know the Berserkers?"

Steve shook his head.

"A local surf gang. Bunch of punks. Show-offs. The leader's this guy Tremor Temchin—you ever hear of him? The story on this dude is that he's got sharks' teeth mounted on the nose of his board so that nobody drops in on him."

"Drops in?"

"Yeah," said Danimal. "Tries to surf a wave

that's his. You do that, and he'll come charging up behind you riding something sharp. The Berserkers are a pretty heavy crew. They used to hang out at Hammerhead—that's a nice break, but nobody else has surfed it for years. Everybody's afraid to. These guys are really territorial."

"Okay," Steve said.

"So I make my way down the cliffs, and when I get down to the beach, somebody's spray-painted a Viking helmet on a boulder."

"That somebody being one of the Berserkers," Steve said.

"No doubt," Danimal said. "The helmet's their logo."

Steve noted that in his book.

"So I paddle out," Danimal says. "There's already about six or seven of these Berserkers in the lineup, and when they see me coming, they start hooting at me, telling me to go home and calling me the Malman."

"The Malman?"

"A Mal's a longboard—it's an old-school board, the kind of board the guys rode in the sixties. The Berserkers are a bunch of hotdoggers—they all ride shortboards. Shortboarders are always trash-talking longboarders."

"Right," said Steve.

"So these guys start snaking my waves, dropping in on me, and edging me out of the lineup. I can't catch a ride. They're acting like Mímulo's their spot, which is nuts. I've been surfing there since I was a kid. The whole thing was bumming me out, so I paddled in after less than an hour. And when I get back up to the car, these punks have waxed my windows and stolen my other board off the roof rack."

"Waxed your windows?"

"Yeah, you rub surf wax all over the glass. Classic trick. It's a total pain to get the stuff off. But the *board*, little man. You don't steal a guy's board."

Steve took his feet off the table. He bit his thumbnail. "Why not go to the cops?" Steve asked.

"I did. They don't care. I can't prove these guys took the board," Danimal said. "But I know they did. About fifteen minutes into my session, one of the younger guys paddled in. He must have been the one who stole it. But the cops just took a crime report and said they didn't have much hope. The police here don't care what happens on the water, man."

"So you want me to be a go-between?" Steve asked. "Bargain for your board back? These guys don't sound like they're real negotiators."

"I don't care how you do it," Danimal said. "Steal

the board back, or just prove that they took it and we can take the evidence to the cops."

"Hmm," said Steve. "What does the board look like?"

"She was beautiful," Danimal said. "About ten feet long, with rounded edges. Single fin. Redwood stringer—a half-inch wood plank running down the whole length of the board. Bright red."

Steve wrote down everything Danimal said although he didn't understand most of it. When he finished, he rocked back and forth in his chair. These Berserkers were bullies, and bullies were high on the list of the Bailey Brothers' most-hated finks. (They were somewhere below cat burglars, but above safecrackers.) In fact, Shawn and Kevin mentioned how much they hated bullies in practically every Bailey Brothers book—they denounced bullies almost as often as they made jokes about Ernest eating too many sandwiches.

"Steve," Danimal said. "You have to get the board back. My grandpa shaped it himself. I love that thing." He looked near tears.

Steve stopped rocking. "I'll take your case."